MISS RIDDELL AND THE PET THEFTS

AN AMATEUR FEMALE SLEUTH HISTORICAL COZY MYSTERY

P.C. JAMES

Miss Riddell and the Pet Thefts Copyright © 2023 by P.C. James

All rights reserved.

No part of this book may be reproduced in any form or by any electronic or mechanical means, including information storage and retrieval systems, without written permission from the author, except for the use of brief quotations in a book review.

This is a work of fiction. Names, places, characters, and incidents are either the product of the author's imagination or are used fictitiously, and any resemblance to any actual persons, living or dead, organizations, events, or locales is entirely coincidental.

For more information:

email: pcjames@pcjamesauthor.com

Facebook: https://www.facebook.com/pauljamesauthor

✾ Created with Vellum

1

NORTH RIDING OF YORKSHIRE, ENGLAND. SUMMER – 1958

PAULINE LOVED THE FARMHOUSE GARDEN, which her parents tended so earnestly to provide fruit and vegetables for their family. Sitting in the sunshine, with the scent of herbs and the song of birds for company, was the perfect antidote to her days spent in smoke-filled offices. She didn't mind the smell of tobacco, she just wished they'd go outside to smoke. Every evening when she got home, she had to hang her clothes to air and wash her hair to get rid of the smell.

"Pauline," Mrs. Riddell said, arriving with a basket to pick raspberries, and interrupting Pauline's reverie. "Will you speak to Jane? Your father and I have tried but she just won't listen."

Jane was the youngest of the Riddell children and Pauline's sister. Though there were only eight years between them, somehow it felt like they were from two different times. Jane's life revolved around popular songs, films, and the latest fashions in hair and clothes. Pauline couldn't share her interest in any of them.

"Jane and I never have a word to say to each other,

Mum," Pauline said. "She won't listen to me. I'm too old, in her eyes."

"She might this time," Mrs. Riddell said. "She's got her 'A' levels and can go to university. You're doing well in your career; maybe she'll respond to that and take your advice."

Her parents, Mrs. Riddell, in particular, wanted Jane to follow an academic path to success. But even Pauline's father was anxious for his daughters to do well and not just become a farmer's wife. The world was opening up and the Riddells were clever; they could do things beyond the circles of work in the Dales.

"I'll try, Mum," Pauline said, "but she's headstrong and stubborn and pushing her may well send her in the opposite direction from the one we want." Pauline was nervous about this request. She knew better than her mother, the friction between herself and Jane. Pauline had 'an old head on her young shoulders' people would say even when she was a child. Jane seemed like she'd never grow up.

"Just make it a conversation," her mother advised. "You must have to deal with awkward so-and-sos where you work."

Pauline laughed. "They're easier to persuade than our Jane has ever been."

Over the weekend, Pauline discovered Jane had applied to universities, as her parents wanted, but was working in a pet shop and grooming business to earn some money. The shop belonged to Jane's best friend's parents and Jane loved it there. All she could talk about was becoming a pet groomer.

"Why not do veterinary studies at university?" Pauline asked, hoping to steer the conversation to where she knew her mother wanted.

"Vets stick their fingers and arms up animals' bums,"

Jane laughed. "How is that anything like clipping their coats?"

"It isn't, of course," Pauline said, "but you would be working with animals and using your brain as well. You'll soon tire of clipping coats and claws; you know you will."

"Last week," Jane said, "we went to Skelsdale Hall and clipped Lady Cecilia's Russian Samoyed. We made more money that afternoon than Dad makes in a week."

"But rich people's dogs aren't groomed every week," Pauline protested, "and there are lots of other people who groom them. Dog groomers aren't among the country's wealthiest citizens, Jane."

"I bet they are in London," Jane replied. "That place is crawling with rich people and their dogs. I bet down there, pet groomers are richer than vets."

Pauline realized the conversation was developing that nervous edge all her conversations with Jane had. "Well, think about it. You know how disappointed Mum and Dad will be if you don't go to university."

"More years of sitting behind a desk might suit you, Pauline," Jane mocked her, "but I want to live now. Everywhere except here, people are partying. We're still up to our bums in mud and I want no part of it." She was almost yelling now.

Pauline, already in her thirties and long out of college, felt ancient in the face of such passion. Passion she'd never felt. Even as a young woman, the dances and parties Pauline had attended weren't the kind Jane longed for. Her engagement to Stephen, cut short when he was killed in Korea, had been wonderfully peaceful. A feeling they were meant for each other without the wild histrionics novels or movies portrayed.

"There'll be parties at university, Jane, you'll see. Mum and Dad only want what's best for you."

"It's my life, not theirs – or yours," Jane said, gesturing to Pauline to go before flouncing off into the yard to fuss over the dogs.

Pauline watched her go with regret. Jane was clever and attractive, her honey-blonde hair was always styled after whatever film star was in fashion. This week it was Leslie Caron in *Gigi*, her clothes too were the very latest thing, though where she got the money for them Pauline didn't want to guess. For dances in the village hall Jane usually wore dresses, home-made like everyone else's, but today she was in her favored American denim jeans. Her clear skin, with just a sprinkling of freckles across her nose, and ice blue eyes, were true Yorkshire; a legacy from all those Vikings of centuries gone by.

Sadly, the teenage rebellion that Pauline was reading so much about in the news was raging in Jane and her choices in almost everything were growing more expensive, which was difficult for her parents to afford on a small family farm income. Half the arguments Jane had with her parents came down to her friends having more than she had. Deflated, Pauline made her way back to the house knowing she'd once again widened the yawning gap between herself and her youngest sister. It had been so easy when Jane was a toddler, she'd followed her older sisters everywhere wanting to be part of everything they did. Now, Jane had no time for any of them nor her parents. Jane would soon storm out of the home. Pauline was sure of it; she hoped today's 'conversation' wasn't what pushed her over the edge. As she'd warned her mother, her meetings with Jane had always been a series of sharp stabbing sentences that didn't flow or fit together to make a conversation.

2

NEWCASTLE-UPON-TYNE, ENGLAND – JULY 1964

EARLY RETIREMENT, thought Chief Inspector Ramsay, was as boring as he'd imagined it would be. It was eight am on a beautiful summer's morning and he was enjoying the short hot spell – four days long now – in the garden of his small semi-detached house. He'd finished reading his morning newspaper. The grass was cut only yesterday; the floral borders of the short path from the house to the gate were weeded the day before, and the house was cleaner than it had ever been. Ramsay's retirement was only one month old. He picked up the library book he'd taken out the night before, mainly for the title, which was *As I Walked Out One Midsummer Morning* and frowned in thought as he read it again.

Unlike the book's author, Laurie Lee, Ramsay wasn't considering walking out to join the Republicans in the Spanish Civil War, but he was thinking that just walking would be better than sitting staring at the walls or the sky. And if he didn't do something active soon, he'd get fat. Not a little overweight, as he was now, but seriously obese. Most of his life, he'd been mildly amused by the bearded civil servants, and they were almost always office-bound public service workers, who spent their time away from work tramping the hills and byways of this green and pleasant land. Now, he wondered if maybe they didn't have a point. He looked at his watch. It wasn't yet nine o'clock and another long day stretched out before him.

The final days at work had been painful for him. Not physically, the wound that had brought an end to his career had healed perfectly well. Only, the police doctor had advised early retirement and his bosses agreed. They had their own reasons for thinking early retirement was a good plan for Chief Inspector Ramsay. He'd constantly forged his own path on investigations. A loose cannon was what many thought of him, Ramsay knew. Their secret animosity made it inevitable they wouldn't take a risk by letting him stay. It had, he knew, started with him letting a young woman, Miss Pauline Riddell, act as an unpaid and unofficial assistant.

Ramsay missed Miss Riddell. He couldn't deny it. In some way, she'd taken the place of the wife and children he'd lost in the war. When she sent him a letter congratulating him on his retirement and wishing him well, it'd been a struggle, a heartache, even, for him to respond. They'd never investigate together again. She had a new job and was now living too far away for them to collaborate. And retired, he no longer had access to unusual problems where her imagination could help.

Ramsay vaguely wondered if he should post an advertisement in the papers as an investigator. To do that, he'd need to be a private detective and that he couldn't face. As a policeman, he'd considered them as an underclass of the justice system. One that was almost wholly focused on divorces and providing evidence of adultery. No. He couldn't do that. Other people's failed love lives were never going to be his business. He now understood Miss Riddell's reluctance to be part of anything sordid, as she would put it. In fact, he didn't want to be part of any investigation right now; it was too soon.

Which brought him back to the book he was holding and its title. Why not 'walk out one midsummer morning'? The answer, of course, was because he'd always been sarcastic about hiking, that's why.

Ramsay frowned. Retirement had been thrust upon him so suddenly, so quickly, he hadn't had time to prepare. He had no hobbies, no interests beyond crime detection, no pastimes beyond brooding and Scotch whisky, no family beyond those in the graveyard he rarely visited, and now he had no colleagues to talk to. Maybe nature, serene restful nature, could replace all those shortfalls in his life. Even his boss had suggested it, he recalled...

"Look, Ramsay, it's for your own good. The doc says so and we can't argue with him, can we?" the chief commissioner had said, when he broke the bad news to Ramsay.

"If I'm happy to go on, and I put that in writing, I can't see how my continuing in the force would be such a problem," Ramsay had countered. "After all, I've no family to complain if I die on the job."

The Commissioner frowned. "I'm sorry, Chief Inspector. The doc won't pass you as fit for duty and that's that. See sense, man. That bullet collapsed one lung and grazed your heart. You need to take the rest of your life at an easy pace. Walk on the beach or on the moors. Enjoy this beautiful world in the years you have left."

They'd been adamant and Ramsay was now retired. Being told to spend the rest of his life walking had been a bitter blow. Of all the pastimes he despised, rambling was very near the top. After rowdy soccer fans, ramblers trespassing on private land leading to complaints from the landowners was one of the constant annoyances of police life. Well, he didn't need to trespass. He could just follow the signposted trails and maybe nature would revive his interest in life.

It might be good for his figure, he thought with a smile. The phrase, so common among women nowadays, aligned with his own thoughts while studying his middle-aged body in the mirror. The one good thing being shot had done for him was he'd lost weight. Days in the hospital followed by weeks of convalescence had reduced his appetite and he'd slowly approached a more sensible looking torso. Looking at himself in the mirror, he was mildly proud of his looks. If he wasn't to return to the shape he'd been, he would have to do something. So why not go walking on the fells, upland moors, and highlands of the country? The sun on his face and the wind in his hair, he was also pleased he still had some of that too, would be the start of a new life. One where he looked on the better side of the world and not its criminal side.

3

RAMSAY FINDS A FRIEND

Ramsay entered the farmyard carefully, avoiding the wet, viscous patties of cow dung that littered the entrance. Clearly, a herd of cows had just passed this spot. On their way to the milking shed, he assumed, though he knew nothing of farming.

There was no one in the yard but a black and white dog, which he recognized as a Border Collie, who leapt to her feet and came to confront him. It was a her, he knew, for in leaping up she'd shaken off four young puppies who were upset at having their morning snack disrupted. They added to her loud barking with high pitched yapping of their own.

A woman came out of the farmhouse door he'd been heading to in hopes of directions, and possibly the chance to buy something fresh for his lunch.

"Hello," Ramsay called, unwilling to pass the still growling dog and her pups who'd trotted to join her. To be honest, he thought wryly, the pups' presence rather detracted from their mother's guard dog stance. They looked too friendly.

"This is private property," the woman said to Ramsay. "Quiet, Bess," she said to the dog.

"I've become a bit lost," Ramsay said. This wasn't entirely true. He was completely lost. "I wondered if you could point me back to the track up Cheviot?"

The woman laughed. "You are a bit lost. Go back the way you came about quarter of a mile and at the fork in the road, go right over the stile."

Ramsay nodded. "I thought that was it. I couldn't buy some bread or meat from you, could I? I also misjudged how hungry I'd get walking up these hills."

The woman looked incredulously at him. "You haven't climbed any hills yet," she said. "Not if you came straight here from Wooler, anyway."

"I did," Ramsay said, embarrassed. "I'm new at rambling, I'm afraid."

She nodded. "You've a long walk ahead of you if you're going to the top of Cheviot."

"A work colleague told me he and his family walked up and down on many a summer day on the weekend," Ramsay said.

"Mebbe they were a bit more used to it than you seem to be," the woman replied, trying not to laugh but only making her amusement more obvious.

Ramsay felt the typical northerner's famous bluntness could be overdone sometimes but he smiled. "I've just retired and thought I'd see something of the country while this good weather lasts. You're right though. I haven't trained properly for this."

She laughed. "I can make you a couple of ham sandwiches if that'll do you."

"That will do nicely, thanks. Can I fill my flask with water too, please?"

She pointed to a tap against the house wall. "Yon water's the same as ours indoors," she said, and returned to the house.

Understanding he wasn't going to be invited inside and offered a seat, Ramsay made his way slowly past the dogs and filled the flask that had held tea before he'd drunk it all at the first mile.

He sat on a large stone and waited while Bess and her pups sniffed and examined him in detail. Ramsay leaned forward and patted Bess carefully. He'd never had a dog but remembered liking them as a child. A memory that gave him a pang of something he couldn't name. Was it regret or just nostalgia?

Bess seemed to like the attention and sat while he stroked her head and scratched under her ears. The pups jostled and tumbled over his shoes, demanding his attention for themselves. He reached out to them, and they licked his fingers in return. Their big eyes held his, locking him into a gentle tussle of their expressions and his hand on their soft, furry bodies. The pups' sharp teeth nipped his skin without ever breaking it as they wriggled and wrangled for position.

He noticed that, of the four pups, one was much smaller than the others. It tried so hard to join in, but the three bigger ones brushed it aside almost as if it weren't there. Ramsay disengaged his left hand and scooped up the little one, placing it gently on his lap.

"Hello, little fellow," Ramsay said, stroking it gently. "You'll have to grow a bit before you can contend with those three." The pup looked at him and Ramsay knew he was lost.

"He'll not grow up," the woman said, approaching Ramsay with his package of sandwiches. "There's no room on a working farm for a useless mouth."

"I see," Ramsay said. "You don't think he's just a slow developer?"

The woman laughed. "We've given him a couple of weeks. His time is up." She handed over the sandwiches. "That's five bob," she said.

Ramsay drew coins from his pocket and handed her two half-crowns. "Can I take this little fellow too?"

The woman took the coins and slipped them into her blouse top. Ramsay guessed they'd gone into her bra where they might stay, safely out of her husband's prying eyes. "If you're quick," she said. "My man's in the milking shed right now but if you're gone before he comes out, you can have the puppy for free."

Ramsay thanked her, rose to his feet, placed the pup in a side pocket of his rucksack and carefully set off out of the yard. When he arrived back at the fork in the road where he'd made his wrong turn, he found he was still expecting to hear an irate farmer demanding payment for a pup the man would soon have drowned. As Ramsay climbed the stile and set out once again for the hilltop, he took the puppy out of the pocket where it was watching the world go by without a hint of concern at leaving its family and said, "So, young fellow, what do I call you?"

The puppy licked his face.

"I don't think any of the thoughts conjured up by that suggest a decent name," Ramsay said, ruffling the fur on the puppy's head. "It must be a name that goes with the new me. The me that strides out in the world and communes with nature," Ramsay continued, placing the puppy into his jacket pocket on the side away from his sandwiches. He looked about. "Bent trees," he mused, "mountain stream, boggy meadow, reeds, clover," he paused, "no that's a girl's name. What will it be?"

The answer still hadn't presented itself when they left the trees in the valley and Ramsey saw before him open hilltops ahead. He realized the woman was right. His colleague, a young wiry man in his thirties, and the man's family, were clearly able to make better time than he was doing. He couldn't even see the summit. He was sweating profusely, and it was approaching midday. A large boulder at the side of the track invited him to stop and rest, so he did.

Taking his sandwiches from one pocket and his new walking companion from the other, he ran his sleeve over his brow to wipe away the sweat that was making his eyes sting. He took off his flat cap and used it as a fan, while the puppy stumbled around in the tussocks of coarse grass and bracken that were too big for him to walk through.

"Bracken," Ramsay said, opening his flask in preparation for a cooling drink. "That's what I'll call you, though, of course, I think you should rightly be an autumn brown to be called that. With your black-and-white colors, I could call you magpie, but it wouldn't be right, would it? You're not a bird nor a football team."

The puppy, sensing he was being talked to, began making his way back to Ramsay, mewing almost like a cat.

"You want water too," Ramsay said, pouring some into his cupped hand. "It's a hot day, all right."

Bracken lapped the water greedily while Ramsay remained stooped, pondering. Was the pup old enough to eat solid food? Had he saved the dog from drowning only to have him die of starvation?

When the pup had finished drinking, Ramsay wiped dry his hand and opened the sandwiches wrapped in waxed paper. They were real man sandwiches, thick slices of homemade bread, lots of farmhouse butter, and a single thick piece of home-cooked ham sliced straight from the bone. He took a bite and smiled beatifically as he chewed. Heaven. Then his eyes caught Bracken's mournful expression and he paused in mid-chew. Ramsay broke off a small piece of bread and gave it to the puppy, who swallowed it in one gulp.

"Hmm," Ramsay said. "Now I don't know if you can chew things or not. Nor do I know if your insides can digest them." He sighed, while Bracken looked hopefully at him.

"No," Ramsay said. "Nothing more until we're home, and I can give you milk or puppy dog food – if there is such a thing."

Bracken continued looking hopeful.

Ramsay took another bite of his sandwich, wrapped the package tightly, placed it in his pocket and said, "Which means we're heading home now." He picked up Bracken, who licked his buttery fingers.

Before arriving home, Ramsay stopped at a nearby pet shop where he learned from the owner that Bracken wouldn't be ready for solid foods for about two weeks if he was only two weeks old.

"Can I bottle feed him cow's milk?" Ramsay asked, seriously alarmed.

"You could try but I have a better solution," the man said. "One of my regular customers has a bitch who lost half her litter to a vicious dog. I'm sure your pup would be welcome there. I can ask if you want?"

"Please do," Ramsay said, "he's already hungry, I think."

"Wait a minute," the shop owner said. He stepped through the doorway separating the shop from the house and called for someone. In a moment, a teenage girl appeared, and he said, "Doris, watch the shop while I take this gentleman along to Mrs. Blackford's house."

Ramsay, carrying Bracken, hurried behind the shopkeeper along a street of sooty red-brick houses until they arrived at the end house of the terrace. The shopkeeper knocked and an elderly woman came to the door. After a brief exchange of greetings and an explanation, Ramsay and Bracken were invited to enter.

Bracken and the nursing mother, a beagle, Ramsay thought, took a moment to become confident in each other before he joined two other puppies at her nipples.

"Well," Mrs. Blackford said, "they'll be quiet for a while. Would you like some tea? I was just about to make a pot."

As they waited for the kettle to boil, Ramsay explained how he came to be the owner of Bracken.

"You did right," Mrs. Blackford said. "Farmers are so cold toward animals and think nothing of killing them. I know it's how they must be to do their jobs, but it upsets me to think of it."

Ramsay agreed, and then asked, "Will it really be no trouble to have me bringing Bracken here for feeding? Won't your husband mind?"

"I'm a widow," Mrs. Blackford said, "and I'd be happy to have a regular visitor. I'm sure Abby would too." She smiled at Abby who was gently licking her two remaining pups as they suckled.

"I'm only two streets away," Ramsay said. "I can bring Bracken early in the morning, take him out throughout the day, and take him home each night. If that would help. I don't want us to become a burden."

Mrs. Blackford shook her head. "He'll be hungry through the night. Leave him here for the first week or so and call in regularly to get him used to you. He'll be no more trouble than our missing two would have been."

It was decided and for the following weeks Ramsay went around to the Blackford house to walk and play with

Bracken, which naturally meant he walked out with Mrs. Blackford and Abby too. It made him uncomfortable. He'd grown so used to his solitary life he found taking account of others faintly disturbing. His relief was enormous when Bracken began eating more solid food and spent more time with Ramsay. It was ungrateful of him, and unfair, but a huge relief, nevertheless.

Bracken had grown larger during this time and bounded ahead of Ramsay whenever they walked. Everything was interesting to Bracken. He stopped at trees, lampposts, street corners, went to meet complete strangers, and tried to become friends with every passing dog or child, leading Ramsay to talk to more people in a single walk than he was used to speaking to in a week.

"Bracken," Ramsay said, as they parted from a particularly garrulous dog owner Bracken had made friends with, "we're going back to walking in nature. All this walking has got me thinking I can get to the top of Cheviot and back without any problem."

Bracken barely heard him; he was straining at his leash to get to something interesting on a nearby lamppost.

When they returned home, Ramsay turned on the radio just as the evening newscaster pronounced the following day would be warm and dry, as a late summer day should be.

"Tomorrow it is," Ramsay said to Bracken, who was asleep on Ramsay's lap and had been for an hour now. Ramsay wasn't sure how much longer he could stay motionless, but he hated to disturb the little thing's rest. Retirement was awakening many such feelings he thought had been lost.

4

RAMSAY IS OFFERED A PUZZLE

Ramsay and Bracken set out from Middleton heading for the summit of Cheviot. He'd learned from his last visit how far Wooler was from his destination. As his hike took him past the farm where Bracken's family lived, he pondered whether he should visit. Would Bracken be upset about being forced to leave his mother again? Would his mother and siblings welcome or refuse Bracken now, considering him an outsider entering their territory? He'd almost decided that he wouldn't visit when he saw the farmer's wife in the yard and Bracken's family around her.

When he reached the fork in the trail that took hikers up to Cheviot's summit or down to the farm nestled in the narrow valley, he took the path to the farm.

"If they don't welcome us, Bracken," he said to the puppy, who was trotting by his side, "we can always leave before we're entangled."

Approaching the farmyard gate, he saw the woman watching him and called, "Hello, there. Remember me?"

"Aye, I do," she replied. "You're the man who took the runt of the litter."

"And I've brought him so you can see how well he's turned out," Ramsay said. Even as he was speaking, Bracken slipped through the five-bar gate and ran to his mother. Ramsay was relieved to see she seemed to recognize him at once. She licked Bracken's face repeatedly as the puppy played about her.

"He looks well," the woman said. "Come in," she added, seeing Ramsay hesitating about opening the gate.

Ramsay did as he was bid and closed the gate carefully behind him. By now all the puppies were playing around their mother in a joyous wriggling of bodies. Ramsay felt an ache beginning in his heart as he watched. It seemed unlikely he could take Bracken away again.

"I hope you won't want to keep him," Ramsay said, glancing at the woman nervously.

"Nay, lad," she said. "He's half the size of the others and will never be big enough to manage the sheep on the tops."

Ramsay looked closely and saw she was right. Bracken had grown but he was still undersized. That should have been upsetting, to know his pet wasn't quite right, but it was reassuring to know he'd have no objection from the humans when he came to leave.

"I set off earlier and parked nearer today," Ramsay said. "This time I mean to reach the top of the mountain."

"Is it a mountain?" the woman asked. "We always call them hills."

"It's over twenty-six hundred feet high so I consider it a mountain," Ramsay said, grinning. "Whatever it may say on the map and in the guidebooks."

The woman nodded. "Did you want sandwiches again?"

Ramsay had brought lunch but realized she may welcome the extra money that selling sandwiches to hikers brought in. "If it isn't any trouble," he said. "You have wonderful fresh bread here."

"It should be," she said. "I make it every morning. The butter and ham are also our own."

"You're very fortunate to be able to make your own food," Ramsay said. "In the city, nothing tastes quite as I remember it as a child."

"Then you play with the dogs," she said, "and I'll make you some lunch just as you remember it."

As she turned to go, Bracken trotted up to Ramsay and nudged his leg with his nose. Ramsay looked down at the puppy's expressive gaze and asked, "What is it, Bracken?"

Bracken turned and walked some steps before stopping to see if he was being followed. Finding he wasn't, he returned and tugged at Ramsay's pant leg.

"He wants to introduce you to the family," the woman said, smiling. "Be polite."

Ramsay followed Bracken across the yard and crouched on his haunches to stroke Bracken's mother and he soon had the whole pack of puppies jostling to be next. He felt tears pricking his eyes and the ache in his heart grew stronger. This family reunion reminded him he could never be reunited with his own and the pain was extreme.

By the time the woman returned with his sandwiches wrapped in newspaper, the dogs had settled down and Bracken was sitting at Ramsay's side.

"You've been adopted," the woman said as she approached.

Ramsay blinked away tears that were still threatening to spill over his eyelids and rose to his feet. "You're right," he said. "I do think I've been entered into the family." He took the sandwiches she offered and slipped them in the small knapsack he'd brought to carry his lunch and flask of tea.

"I didn't think you'd be able to get up," the woman said. "I thought you'd need a hand."

Ramsay grinned. "I've put on some pounds over the years," he said, "but I always passed the annual fitness test. Now I'm retired, I'm going to lose the last of those pounds, which is why I'm experimenting with hiking."

"Were you in the police?" she asked, her expression serious.

"I was, yes," Ramsay said. "I hope that doesn't mean you want your sandwiches back." He smiled to show her he was joking, though he knew many people had mixed feelings about the police.

She shook her head. "It's just we have a puzzle and someone who understands crime may be able to help."

Ramsay didn't like the sound of this and said, "If you know of a crime, you should inform the police."

"Oh, it isn't really a crime," she said. "At least, not yet."

This is how Miss Riddell kept being drawn into investigations, Ramsay thought. I should leave quickly before my resolve to break from the past weakens.

"Then what is it?" he found himself asking.

"My mother has lost a pet," the woman said.

"A pet? Not her pet?"

"It's my brother's pet and it was staying with my mother," the woman said.

"I can see how that would be difficult," Ramsay agreed. "That sort of thing can cause ill feelings in the best of people."

The woman nodded. "But it's more than that. The cat is a star and is worth a lot to my brother. In fact, it's his livelihood now."

Ramsay was puzzled. "How can that be?"

"You'll have heard of Mittens, I'm sure," she said. "Mittens the kitten?"

Ramsay shook his head.

"You have no children then," the woman said.

The ache in Ramsay's heart sprang back into excruciating life. "No," he said. "I have no children."

"Mittens has been a star on Children's Radio Hour for a year now and she's about to move onto television and there's talk about a film."

Ramsay was puzzled. "If Mittens has been on radio for a year, she can hardly still be a kitten."

"I don't know the details," she said. "I imagine they will manage to explain."

Ramsay agreed they would, and continued, "Still, this is a job for the police, not an amateur sleuth. They have the resources that ordinary people don't have."

"They also have real crimes to investigate, or so they told my mother when she contacted them. They added Mittens to their list of missing pets."

"Surely the television company will pay a reward or hire detectives, if Mittens is such a big star," Ramsay said.

The woman shook her head. "They say there are plenty of cats with white front paws, which by the way is how it came to be called Mittens."

Ramsay nodded. "I guessed. And it's true there are plenty of cats with white paws. I imagine they might train several white-pawed cats to do any tricks needed to make it look like they were being intelligent for the purposes of the story."

"So, you can see why my brother is so desperate. Right now, he and Mittens are on the road to television stardom and even wealth. Instead, with her gone, he could be back on the dole."

"Surely he could find another Mittens, as easily as the television company could?"

"Of course, and he's looking for one right now, but Mittens isn't just his stage prop. He loves that cat."

Ramsay frowned. That did tug his heartstrings. Losing a loved one was something he could understand.

"Couldn't you just talk to my brother and mother? It would mean a lot."

Ramsay hesitated. This was the moment to say no if he was to throw off detecting for at least the near future.

"On the understanding I'm not promising to do anything more than listen," Ramsay said at last.

"I understand," the woman said.

"Where will I find your mother?" Ramsay asked.

"She's in a home outside of Manchester."

"Oh," Ramsay said, shaking his head. "I'm sorry. I took it she was somewhere local. Manchester isn't close. I'd need train fares or petrol money and a place to stay down there. You, and she, would be better off finding someone local to investigate."

"My mother isn't poor," the woman said. "If I talk to her, she may be happy to pay your costs, and even wages."

"What's she doing in Manchester?" Ramsay asked.

"After my dad died, she married again to a farmer down there. He's gone too now, but he owned the farm and she inherited. A neighbor bought it when she became too infirm to manage. She has enough to get by, believe me."

Ramsay thought carefully. He didn't like the idea at all. He was once sent on a training course to Manchester and the memory lingered. Newcastle was sooty, but Manchester was all that and seedy besides. On the other hand, if he was going to 'walk out one midsummer morning' that would surely someday lead to arriving at places he was unfamiliar and uncomfortable with. And at least he'd only be 'near Manchester' and with no one shooting at him, unlike author Laurie Lee's experience.

"Here's my address and my telephone number," Ramsay said. "*If* the cat is still missing when you speak to your mother and *if* she wants me to investigate, get in touch. Now I must go, or I won't have reached the summit before summer is gone."

5

NOT AS SIMPLE AS IT SEEMED

CLIFTON MANOR RESIDENTIAL Home was in a small country village some seven miles outside Manchester. It was a middling sized brick house, probably built for a local man-made-good in Victorian times. Situated on the edge of a village, where most houses were older stone cottages, the house looked like an outsider and probably the owners had been too. Ramsay rang the doorbell and waited. A woman wearing a uniform dress opened the door and asked, "Yes?"

"I'm here to see Mrs. Adelaide Turnbull," Ramsay said. Only just preventing himself from announcing himself as the police.

"Are you a relative?"

Ramsay shook his head. "Her daughter, Jean Fisher, asked me to drop by," Ramsay said. "She thought I might be able to help with the missing cat."

The woman laughed. "If you find it," she said, "I and everyone else here will pay you to keep it."

"Oh, dear. Was it so bad?"

The woman nodded, as she stood aside to let him in. "Many of the residents have pets with them and they're very good. I fear Mittens couldn't accept being separated from her owner and was unhappy in the few days she was here. I hope your puppy," she glanced at Bracken who was looking around for someone to make friends with, "is well trained."

"Bracken is young, but he loves everyone so if he gets off the leash, he'll only lick your residents to death. He even likes cats, though he's a bit scared of them."

Bracken's expression of a small dog being unfairly accused confirmed Ramsay's words.

The woman laughed. "He knows how to play to the audience, anyway," she said, bending down to stroke his head. "You don't fool me," she continued, speaking sternly to Bracken. "I have two Jack Russells and when they aren't creating mayhem, they look as innocent as you've just done."

Bracken recognized a friend and grinned at her, while graciously accepting all the caresses she gave him.

"I'll be extra careful," Ramsay said, when they began moving again. As they walked through the building to a wide, south-facing terrace room, Ramsay added, "Mittens may well have just escaped and is on her way back to her own home."

"I think that's the most likely explanation," the woman said, "but you'll never persuade Mrs. Turnbull of it." She led the way to an elderly woman in a wheelchair who was gazing absent-mindedly out of the window into the garden.

"Adie," the nurse said, touching the older woman's shoulder, "you have a visitor."

Adie turned to look at Ramsay. She nodded. "You're the policeman Jeanie told me about."

"I'm a retired policeman," Ramsay said, holding out his hand for hers. "Tom Ramsay. Your daughter thought I might be able to help, or at least set your mind at rest." Her hand was soft, limp in his. He was puzzled. He'd expected a younger woman. The daughter, Jean, couldn't be more than thirty but this woman looked like she was eighty.

Seeing his puzzled expression, Adie said, "I'm ill, not old. Now, how can you help?"

"I won't know until I hear more," Ramsay said, sitting in the chair opposite.

"Then we must wait for my son to arrive. He's on his way. I told him you were coming."

"Was he here when Mittens went missing?" Ramsay asked, puzzled.

"Nay, lad. It was the middle of the night. But he can tell you all about the cat and the ransom demand he's just received."

"Well, while we're waiting, maybe you can tell me about the night Mittens went missing?" Ramsay asked.

The story was easy to tell. Mittens had been roaming Adie's room, as she always did when it was time for bed. She wouldn't sleep in her carrying basket. When Adie woke, Mittens was gone. The door and windows were shut, and the night nurse saw and heard nothing.

"I'll need to speak to the nurse on shift that night," Ramsay said. "Is she here today?"

Adie shook her head. "She's always on nights so she can look after her bairns before and after school."

Before he had time for further questions, Ramsay heard the nurse letting someone in at the front door. He guessed it would be the owner of Mittens.

A minute later, the nurse ushered a short, rotund man into the room. He looked like a bookie's tout, Ramsay thought as he rose and introduced himself.

"Malcom Turnbull," the man said, shaking Ramsay's hand. "Best known as Magic Mal."

"Magic Mal?"

"I started in showbiz as a magician," Mal replied. "It's my stage name. I'm glad you've come; I need all the help I can get."

Ramsay didn't disabuse him but said, "They want money, I hear?"

"Ten thousand pounds," Mal exclaimed. "I don't have that sort of money. People think if you've a show on the BBC, you're a millionaire."

Ramsay smiled. "To be honest, I rather thought that too."

"Well, I'm not," Mal said. "Can you help?"

"I don't know," Ramsay said. "Tell me about you and Mittens. I've never heard of you, I'm afraid."

"As I said, I'm a magician," Mal said, speaking quickly, the words tripping over themselves as he spoke. "I used to do local shows, cabarets, and children's parties. A stray kitten was outside my window one morning, meowing to be let in. It was winter, and she was frozen. I let her in and gave her warm milk. She adopted me." He paused for breath.

"Did you appeal for the owners to claim her?"

"Of course, but you know how it is with cats. There are always more cats than people who want them. Anyway, I was stuck with her, which was all right because I have no family and she filled the hours alone at home."

"I'm the same," Ramsay said. "I got a dog." He ruffled Bracken's head as he spoke.

Mal nodded, smiling. "Mittens is clever and cute," he continued. "One day, when I put down my magician's top hat, she jumped inside. It came to me at once. Every magician pulls a dove out of his hat; my gimmick would be a kitten. That day it was a child's birthday party and they loved her."

"And you've been a team ever since," Ramsay guessed.

"We have. Anyway, at the next children's birthday party I did, one of the parents worked on BBC Radio Newcastle. He asked would I be interested in being on a show. I said, 'How? No one could see me or Mittens on the radio'."

"I'd wondered that."

"Well, he said they'd record Mittens' meows, different ones, you know, and there'd be other sound effects. All I had to do was write a skit that could be done through speech, like any entertainer, and when Mittens was to appear, they would insert the appropriate meow. She has a very distinctive meow, you see. Everyone who has heard her would recognize it."

"I still don't see how a magician with a cat does a show on radio."

"In this case it was more of a comedy sketch," Mal said, "rather than a magic show. But to answer your question, it works the same way a radio drama, or even a storybook, works. The narration and dialogue create pictures in the listeners' minds. Sound effects give the story color."

"And it worked?"

"Much to my astonishment, it did, and I was invited back. That was only a year ago and now we've recorded a television show. It's set to air soon."

"And now Mittens is gone."

"The announcement about the new television show was in the paper about a week ago. Somebody saw it and... Well, here we are."

"Do you have any idea who might be behind this?" Ramsay asked.

"None. Other than the money, it makes no sense," Mal said. "I'm too small an entertainer to have enemies and there's no other man and animal act who lost out when I got hired or is poised to step in."

"What about family or friend friction?"

"I have no family of my own," Mal said. "Mum here is my only parent left and Jeanie, my sister, is my only sibling. Neither of them has anything to gain by this."

"The difficulty, as I see it," Ramsay said, "is that a member of the public might have learned of your new promotion to the world of television, but they wouldn't have known Mittens was staying here with your mum. Why was she here, by the way?"

"I had to go down to London for contract discussions," Mal said. "The show we recorded is a trailer, you understand. If the public like it, there'll be more. I didn't want to take Mittens with me because I was planning to be there for the whole week. I live in a small flat in Manchester now and hardly know my neighbors, they come and go so often. Jeanie has dogs and cats who might not have welcomed Mittens, and she's so far away, so Mum was the best choice. I dropped Mittens off here and went on to London the next day."

Ramsay nodded. He turned to Adie Turnbull and asked, "To confirm, you heard nothing that night. Someone entering your room, for example?"

"Nay, lad. They give me a pill at bedtime and I'm out like a log until morning."

"Mittens was loose in the room, so if someone did enter your room, she could easily have slipped out into the rest of the house," Ramsay said. "Anyone here in the home could have nabbed her, or could they?"

Mal snorted, shaking his head. "Mittens wasn't a cat for cuddling. She'd take her claws to any stranger who tried to pick her up uninvited."

Adie nodded her agreement. "That's true but there were people here she did like."

"Perhaps we could talk to them," Ramsay said.

"We could, only they would also have been asleep in bed," Adie said. "Everyone gets a pill at bedtime."

Ramsay shuddered at the picture that conjured up in his mind, but continued, "They may not have taken their pill, or the night nurse may have become friends with Mittens. After all, she and Mittens had two or three nights to become acquainted."

Adie thought about this. "Certainly, Mittens did accept her when she came into my room on her evening round."

"Then we have a start," Ramsay said. "Only we must be careful how we approach these people. They're probably innocent and, if they take offence at our questions, you, Adie, are the one who must live with them after this is all over."

6

PAULINE GETS A PHONE CALL

"Pauline Riddell," Pauline said, when she picked up the handset.

"It's me, Pauline." Recognizing Freda's voice and the anxious edge in it, Pauline asked, "Is everything all right with Mum?"

"Mum's fine," Freda said. "It's Jane."

Pauline was about to respond derisively, then stopped. Freda sounded so unhappy, this may be more serious than normal and not just the usual boyfriend troubles Jane accumulated. Pauline hadn't seen Jane since their father's funeral the previous year, a death that Pauline placed squarely on Jane's shoulders. Their father had doted on Jane, the youngest in the family, and it broke his heart when she decided to skip university and do pet grooming. Her riotous life in town with other equally unruly teenagers, along with the inevitable visits from the police warning her parents of their daughter's likely end, just added to the stress on her mother and father. No wonder flu had taken her dad to an early grave. Jane had plenty to answer for, but she seemed oblivious to the damage she had done.

"What about Jane," Pauline asked, as evenly as she could.

"She's in hiding," Freda said. "In fear for her life."

"Not from another violent thug she's gone out with for the thrills?" Pauline said, her worst fears realized.

Freda seemed to hesitate, before saying, "It's not like that this time."

"I don't care, Freda," Pauline said. "Since she opened that pet salon in Manchester, it's been one thing after another and all of them have ended with Jane wanting money from us."

"That was years ago, Pauline, and she's really doing well now," Freda replied. "She does all the stars' pets and is raking it in."

"What stars? She's in Manchester, not New York or London."

"You're so out of touch, Pauline. I wonder you can hold down a job in the modern world. Manchester has a great pop scene and movies, too. And then there are footballers."

Pauline groaned. Stars. Entertainers who had a moment in the sun and then disappeared.

"You must have heard of Herman's Hermits? The Hollies?" Freda suggested.

"If I have, I've already forgotten them," Pauline said.

"Or George Best, Denis Law, Bobby Charlton?"

"I've heard of them, yes," Pauline said. "What of it?" One of the dubious benefits of being surrounded by men at work was that she knew more about sports and sports personalities than any sane woman could ever want to know.

"Lots of them, and others, have pets and our sister has become their favorite pet groomer. I know you won't believe it, Pauline, but she's becoming rich out of all this."

"Then she can buy off whatever thug she's been dating,"

Pauline said. "If I judged Manchester by what you've told me of Jane's past boyfriends, I'd have the whole city put in prison."

Freda laughed nervously. "This is different—"

"How different?" Pauline interjected.

"I'm trying to tell you how and you keep stopping me," Freda shouted.

Pauline drew a deep breath and focused. "Very well, tell me and I'll try to listen."

"Jane agreed to take a businessman's wife's dog over last weekend, groom it, and return it Monday when the woman returned from a trip with her husband."

"And?"

"The dog disappeared from Jane's house and the owners received a ransom note. They think Jane is part of it and sent some unpleasant men to her apartment. She saw them coming and ran. She's in hiding. The word is out they're going to torture her until she talks." Freda paused for breath. "The word is there's no guarantee they'll leave her alive after she's talked."

"This must be quite some dog," Pauline said skeptically.

"It's more who the owners are and how much the wife dotes on the dog, apparently," Freda replied.

"I know nothing about dognapping, and little about Manchester or the world these people live in," Pauline said. "She should go to the Manchester police."

"Jane says that isn't a good idea," Freda replied. "The owners and the police chiefs move in the same circles if you understand what I mean."

Pauline nodded. Rumors about corruption in big city police departments were always going the rounds. It was possible some of them were true.

"You want me to investigate," Pauline said, "but I don't

see how that will help. Even if the owners get the dog back, they are unlikely to let Jane go if it's known they've threatened her. They'd lose face and those kinds of people live in a world where that's important to their deranged version of respect."

"They may be merciful if the dog is returned unharmed and without them paying the ransom," Freda said. "You live nearby now and our quarrel with Jane is in the past. Won't you at least try?"

"Forgiveness should only come after a frank admission of wrongdoing on the part of the forgiven," Pauline said. "Jane's predicament is almost certainly the reward for her behavior, which is to say, her own fault."

"How can you say that?" Freda cried.

"Freda. If I agreed to look after someone's dog for a time and the dog was taken and a ransom demanded, the owners would *not* assume I was the one demanding the ransom. I don't behave in ways that would suggest that was something I would do. Nor do you. Nor do many of the millions of other people in the country. But they're sure Jane would do exactly that."

"They're not nice people, Pauline. Jane says he's a gangster. He provides drugs and other illicit goods to the stars."

"He provides evil goods and services to shallow silly people. Jane provides equally useless services to the same set of silly people who are themselves mainly useless and worse, dangerous." Pauline paused to catch her breath. "Freda, the people you're describing, and the world in which they live, are why I don't do sordid crimes."

"But she's our sister, Pauline," Freda said simply. "We can't walk away."

Pauline's shoulders slumped, deflated. "No," she said. Freda was right. "We can't walk away. Where is she?"

"She's hiding out in a friend's caravan."

"That doesn't sound safe," Pauline said. "They'll trace her through the friend."

"Then go and collect her," Freda said. "She'll be safer with you. Nobody knows you're her sister and living nearby."

"Where is she?" Pauline asked. She noted the address and tore the page from the pad. "I'll get her this evening," she continued, "but I doubt I'll be able to help. I'm only just settling in here and I don't know anyone. Also, I fear the dog will be returned, alive or dead, before I've found it because I can't believe the dognappers will keep it very long."

After she'd hung up the phone, Pauline put on a hat and summer jacket before leaving the house. Her new car, not brand new, of course, for even with fees from grateful clients to supplement her wages she couldn't afford new, was parked on the road outside the old Victorian house where she lived. The house was now two flats and Pauline lived in the upper one. She hoped with her increasing responsibility and salary at work, and her fees from her successful investigations, her next home and car would be brand new and her own.

She turned the key and Milly, her almost-new Morris Minor, came to life. She was already in love with the car, naming it after the title character in a favorite children's book – *Milly-Molly-Mandy*. She loved it so much she intended to buy only Morris Minors in the future, and each would be named for the book. Pauline turned Milly out into the road, heading to Manchester to rescue her errant sister.

Arriving at the end of the street Freda had mentioned, Pauline stopped. This was an expensive part of the city outskirts, and the homes were hidden behind leafy hedges and trees. Nevertheless, she knew the occupants would see and recall an unusual car entering their enclosed space. It wasn't a through road, just a short narrow lane ending in a cul-de-sac. Even parked as she was, someone might already be wondering about her presence. She drove on and parked farther along the road that brought her here. Thankfully, for once, it wasn't raining. She stepped out of her car and locked it before setting out in search of the house with the caravan parked in its drive.

7

THE MYSTERY DEVELOPS

THE NURSE who did the night shift arrived at eight o'clock and Ramsay, who'd waited with Adie, introduced himself and his purpose for being there. The woman agreed to chat after she'd met with the dayshift and done her initial rounds of the residents with their nightly medications.

"You want to know about the night Mittens disappeared," the woman said, entering Adie's room with a small tray, a glass of water, and a bowl containing a pill.

"I do," Ramsay said. "I don't know if it will help me, but something might have occurred to explain the catnapping."

"It's ludicrous," the woman said. "Who would steal a cat and who do they think would pay a ransom to get it back?"

"Didn't you like Mittens?"

"I liked her, and she was fine with me," the woman said, "but be sensible, it's just a cat."

"Except this one is a star," Ramsay said.

"I feel guilty about that," the nurse said, frowning. She turned to Adie, saying, "I told people we had a soon-to-be TV star staying here. It may be my fault this happened. I'm sorry if it turns out that way."

"Do you remember who you told?" Ramsay asked.

"My family mainly," the nurse said, "but they're such a bunch of chatterboxes I may as well have told the whole village."

"Is there anyone in the village likely to try and ransom a cat?"

The woman laughed. "We have one old fellow who poaches but he wouldn't have the gumption to do something like this."

Ramsay nodded thoughtfully. The not-so-bright poacher might also not understand he'd asked too much, which was the scariest part of the ransom demand. Ten thousand pounds was ten years' salary for the average man in today's Britain.

"Would this poacher have heard about Mittens, do you think?"

"It's possible. When my hubby Reg gets in the pub, everyone hears our business."

"You can't think how it was done, though?" Ramsay asked. "After all, even if Mittens slipped out of this room when you came in, she couldn't get out of the building, could she?"

The woman shook her head. "It's quiet around here at night but we still lock up the doors and windows when the day staff leave. I'm here on my own with a house full of sleeping guests. Anyway, a catnapper wouldn't hang around outside on the off chance the very cat he wanted would get out."

"True," Ramsay said. "Then she left with the day shift."

"Hey, I didn't say that," the nurse protested.

"If everything is locked, it's the only explanation," Ramsay said. "I don't mean one of them took her, only she left when they did and may be trying to find her way home."

Mollified, the nurse agreed that was the most likely explanation.

Wishing the two women good night, Ramsay was escorted to the door and out. He heard the locks and bolts being turned and slid home. Waiting a moment to see he wasn't being watched, he then set off around the building to assure himself what the nurse said was true. He didn't really doubt it; he'd lock everything too if it were him alone on the night shift. Satisfied that on this night at least, there were no exits available for an adventurous cat, he returned to his car and drove back to the Bed and Breakfast he'd booked into.

* * *

PAULINE KNOCKED on the caravan door and stood back so an occupant could see her out of the window. She was just in time. A lace curtain twitched, two eyes looked briefly out, and a moment later the door opened.

"You got my message then," Jane said, tugging Pauline's jacket collar and dragging her inside.

"We shouldn't waste time talking," Pauline said. "Pack your things and we'll get away from here."

Jane nodded and began grabbing clothes strewn across the chairs and table. She rushed into the caravan's small bedroom and flung them onto the bed.

Pauline shuddered. Jane was as untidy in her habits as she was in her mind. They would struggle to share Pauline's modest apartment. She watched Jane stuff her clothes into a large traveling trunk and sit on the lid while fastening it.

Pauline stepped outside and said, "Wait while I make sure the coast is clear." She hurried to the end of the short driveway and looked up and down the lane. It was quiet and no one was about. She waved for Jane, whose head was poking out through the partly open door, to join her.

Jane stepped out, hauled the trunk to the ground, left it, and ran to the door of the house, pushing the caravan keys through the mailbox flap.

When Jane arrived at her side, Pauline set off at a brisk pace until she realized Jane was struggling with the trunk. She let Jane catch up and they both took up the trunk between them.

"What possessed you to run away from home with this?" Pauline asked, as they wobbled their way to her car.

"I didn't know how long I might have to be away from home so I brought everything I could carry," Jane gasped.

"What's in here?"

"Things," Jane said. "Stuff I need."

With the trunk safely stowed in the back seat, they drove off with Pauline watching her rear-view mirror in case a car was following them out from the lane. It wasn't until they were on the road back to her apartment in Newton Heath that she relaxed enough to talk.

"I want to be clear, Jane," Pauline said. "I've had success in crime solving but nothing like this. I don't know what you're mixed up in, but it is well outside my experience. I'll do what I can, only you shouldn't expect miracles here. You may have to move and live somewhere else at the end of this."

"You'll sort it out," Jane said, grinning. "You always do."

Jane's whole demeanor was one of excitement, which was in complete contrast to the dread Pauline felt.

"Who is this man who's threatening you? Why does he think he can?"

"He's a nasty piece of work," Jane said, though her tone

suggested otherwise. "His wife's great. She and I are best friends."

"Surely then, he wouldn't really harm a best friend of his wife?"

"Wouldn't he though," Jane said, laughing. "You don't know these people."

"I don't understand. If she isn't angry with you, why is he?"

"He's over-protective, thinks she's easily duped, that's all. He'll calm down and we'll all be friends again," Jane said.

"How can you take all this so lightly? Aren't the threats real?" Pauline cried.

"Pauline this is life in the fast lane," Jane said, her words tumbling out. "You'll sort it out or his wife, Wendy, will calm him down. Something will happen and make it right. You'll see."

"And if it doesn't?"

Jane shrugged and laughed. "You know what they say, 'live fast, die young, and leave a good-looking corpse'."

"Is this life so exciting you'd happily die for it?" Pauline asked, bewildered at a view of life so opposite to her own. Jane clearly saw this as an action movie with herself as the star.

"Pauline, I've packed more living into the last three or four years than you will in your whole life. Lives are measured by moments, not by years."

"That's madness, Jane. You know it is, right?'

"You sound drearier with every passing year, Pauline. You're the stereotypical anxious mother without actually having any kids."

They lapsed into a silence that lasted until they arrived at Pauline's apartment. She parked and they carried the trunk from the car, up the narrow stairs to Pauline's rooms.

"The couch pulls out into a bed," Pauline said. "That's yours. I'm keeping my bedroom."

"We could share," Jane protested. "I don't mind."

"I do," Pauline replied bluntly. "And you'll keep your clothes off the furniture while you're here. I don't want to find your undies drying on door handles or anywhere else." Memories of the caravan when first viewed resonated strongly in Pauline's head.

"Then you'd better find Mimi fast," Jane said, smiling, "or get Mother here to tidy up for us."

"Mimi? The dog's called Mimi?"

"Why shouldn't she be? She's the most adorable toy poodle you've ever seen, pure white with a pink bow and matching nails."

"Dogs have claws, Jane, not nails."

Jane laughed. "You never really left the farm, did you? They're all just animals to you."

Pauline changed the subject. "Tea?"

Jane let out a peel of laughter that Pauline felt might have been heard for a mile around. "You're joking. What spirits do you have? I can drink anything."

"I have sherry and nothing else," Pauline said.

Jane shook her head in dismay. "Tell me there's somewhere near here to buy alcohol. I can't drink that muck."

"There's a bottle shop at the bottom of the street," Pauline said. "But I'll go. I don't want you showing your face anywhere until this is cleared up."

"Get me vodka," Jane said. "If I'm stuck in here all day, better get two bottles, full size, not half."

"Have you got money for that?"

"I'll pay you back when I get some cash," Jane said. "I brought my jewelry to pawn but until then I have hardly any cash."

"Get yourself unpacked," Pauline said, "while I'm away." She left the building with dark thoughts running through her head. How was it possible for two siblings to be so unalike?

8

RAMSAY SETTLES INTO THE SEARCH

The bar of the *Maid Marian*, Clifton's village pub, was busy when Ramsay entered. Inside was noisy and smoky, both reasons Ramsay preferred to drink his Scotch at home. Tonight, however, he was searching for Reg or, better, the poacher, Harold. He ordered a pint of bitter and, while the barman pulled his pint, asked if either of the men was in. The barman continued pulling the pint in silence. Ramsay watched the glass overflowing with foam and wondered what was wrong with the beer. He'd never seen anything like it.

Finally, when the glass had a fair measure of beer and a rapidly settling foam, the barman said, "I'm not sure who you mean, sir. We have several Regs and Harolds and a lot of folks who aren't regulars in tonight. You'd best ask around."

Ramsay paid him and turned to the crowd, many of whom were observing him suspiciously. A stranger in a village pub was always an event. In a dark corner sat a small, wiry man sipping a pint. His eyes darting lizard-like to-and-from Ramsay. Ramsay grinned. Criminals could sense a copper without needing to see a warrant card and the reverse was also true. He made his way through the crowd to where the man was sitting.

"Can I join you?" Ramsay asked, sitting on the bench beside him.

"It's a free country," the man said.

"So, they say," Ramsay agreed. "Are you Harold?"

"Is that what he said?" The man gestured at the barman who was watching them intently.

"He said nothing," Ramsay said. "I understand you're out late of an evening, did you see the cat that went missing?"

"I don't know nothing about no cat," the man said. 'And I ain't Harold, neither."

"That's a shame," Ramsay said. "There's money in it for anyone who helps find it."

"I never heard that," the man said, his interest piqued.

"You have now."

"How much?"

"So, you did see something," Ramsay said.

"Might have. I couldn't rightly say. Could be nothing, but who knows?"

"I could go as high as ten shillings for good information," Ramsay said. The man licked his lips, his anticipation of drinks to come was so strong.

"Not here," the man said. "By the lane end in an hour."

Ramsay sighed. He didn't want to spend another minute in the room, but he understood the man's desire not to be thought of as passing information to the police. There may be bigger fish than Harold in the room and they wouldn't be kind to an informer.

"I'll finish my pint and leave," Ramsay said. "You can follow later but not too much later."

The man nodded and they drank in companionable silence until Ramsay declared himself done. "By the way," he said, as he rose from the bench, "is the local beer always this frothy?"

The man shrugged. "Don't know what you mean," he said. "It's the same as other beers, ain't it?"

Ramsay shook his head. "Not the ones I'm used to. Well, good night. It was nice talking to you." He wended his way through the crowd and out into the street. His car was at the wrong end for his clandestine meeting, so he moved it and settled down to wait.

DUSK WAS WELL advanced when he saw his informant leave the pub and walk toward him, watching carefully to see he wasn't being observed.

Ramsay stepped out of his car and joined the man in the darker shadows of a nearby building.

"Well?" he asked.

"Ten bob," the man said.

"I'll give you five shillings now," Ramsay said, "and the rest if I think it's worth it."

The man accepted that and waited while Ramsay counted out the coins from his pocket. When the man had the money, he said, "I did see summat that night." He paused, looked around before continuing, "A car and a man."

"Who was the man?"

"Don't know. He weren't someone local."

"And the car?"

"A big one," the man said. "That's why I noticed. Not your ordinary runabout."

"Did you recognize the make, see the color, a license plate?"

"It were black and looked like an Austin A60 but flasher," the man said.

"And the man?"

"Not from round here, well-built, flash-dresser, looked like a movie gangster," the man said.

"Fair hair, dark?"

"Dark, I think, though it was getting to sunset and dusk," the man said.

"How did he catch the cat?"

"I don't know that he did," the man replied, "but he was parked nearby and waiting for something. There's nothing up that way but the residential home so I reckon he was the one after the cat."

Ramsay nodded. "There's nothing else you can tell me about the man, his car, or that night?"

The man frowned. "This isn't summat I saw, only my thoughts on what I saw. The man was no amateur catnapper. He's not one of the residential home women's husbands, nothing like that. If he took the cat, it's bigger. A real operation."

"Sounds unlikely," Ramsay said and was amused to see the angry expression descend on his informant's face at his thoughts being rejected. Ramsay laughed. "Still, it is good information. I'll give you a ten-shilling note, give me back my coins."

The exchange was made, and his informant slipped silently away around a corner with a high wall and was lost to sight.

As he drove back to the B&B, Ramsay reviewed the evidence he'd accumulated. The man with the big car may have nothing to do with the disappearance of Mittens but his being there was strangely coincidental if he hadn't.

9

PAULINE SEARCHES FOR CLUES

WITH SEVERAL VODKAS INSIDE HER, Jane was even more excited than she'd been sober. She really did see herself as being in a movie. Pauline was horrified, realizing she could never keep her indoors or away from danger for the length of time an investigation would take.

"Tell me again how the dog went missing?" Pauline asked, hoping the drink would stir memories in Jane's befuddled brain.

"Mimi was in my flat, which was locked, and I was at a party," Jane said. "There I've told you again. Happy now?"

"No, I'm not," Pauline replied. "You say there was no forced entry so how did the dognapper get in or the dog get out?"

"People have a key," Jane said, unconcerned.

"What people?" Pauline cried, exasperated.

"My friends," Jane said. "They come and go, as I do at their places. It's what we do. We share."

Pauline felt there was little point asking for a list of Jane's friends. They could have passed the key to *their* friends and on and on until half the foolish people in this social world would be suspects.

"Was there nothing to indicate who'd been into your place?" Pauline asked.

"Nothing," Jane said. "All that was missing was Mimi."

"What did the police say?"

"They put Mimi on their list of missing pets and promised to look out for her," Jane replied. "I explained she hadn't run away – that she'd been kidnapped. It did no good."

"And you didn't tell them whose dog it was?"

"Too right, I didn't. Tosh wouldn't want the police looking closely at him or his wife," Jane said.

"Why do you associate with people like this?" Pauline asked. She was both fascinated and repulsed by the life Jane described.

"I've been to Paris, Monte Carlo, and Rome with Wendy and Mimi, Pauline. Where have you been? Newcastle and now the unfashionable outskirts of Manchester."

Pauline reddened. "When I see those other places, it will be in the company of decent people or by myself," she said. "Not with drug dealers and gangsters."

Jane shrugged. "They provide things people want. Isn't that what we're told is the path to prosperity?"

"Drugs kill people!"

"In this country, we never had problems with people taking drugs," Jane said. "One day, we'll go back to that because it is what people want and it's not the law's business what people do with themselves. When the law goes back to how it was, you'll say it's fine."

"I will not," Pauline replied. "The law is often an ass and new instances of that won't change my mind."

"I've also been to some seriously groovy parties," Jane

said mischievously, seeing her sister becoming more agitated with each passing minute. "You wouldn't believe what goes on there."

"Can we return to the night the dog went missing?"

Jane yawned. "I'm bored with that. Where can we go tonight?"

"We're going nowhere," Pauline said. "Who knew the dog was Wendy's dog?"

"I told you this already," Jane complained. "Anyone who's anyone in Manchester knows Wendy and Mimi."

"Business rivals?"

Jane laughed, genuinely amused. "His last business rival is under a bridge support of the new M6 motorway being built, so they say." She frowned. "Though I hear there's a new rival on the other side of the river."

"Does this new one have a name?"

"Yes, but I don't know for sure. I'll have to check," Jane said. "But Pauline, it makes no sense. People this high up in the world don't do childish crimes."

"I'm sure you're right but my point still stands. They do have enemies."

"Yes, but not ones mad enough to steal Mimi and leave Tosh alive to find them."

"You've never mentioned me to them, have you?" Pauline asked, a new concern flitting into her mind.

"Don't be daft," Jane said. "They wouldn't be interested in a provincial nobody like you or any of my dull as dishwater family."

Pauline stared at her, hoping to see from Jane's expression this was true. All she saw was Jane fiddling with her glass and avoiding Pauline's eyes. Pauline felt certain Jane had regaled Wendy with plenty of stories about her 'dull as dishwater family' over the past years. Both women would have enjoyed gossiping about the nobodies they'd left behind, contrasting their families' miserable lives with the glamor of the big city life they enjoyed. She could only hope Jane had given no clues as to where her family lived.

Pauline asked, "Then we won't be hearing our mother is being held captive somewhere to be exchanged for you?"

Jane's already pale face turned white. "I can't remember everything I've said these past years. It wouldn't matter, though, Wendy's so out of it on pills and gin she wouldn't remember."

Pauline's insides grew more uncomfortable with every word of Jane's prevarication.

"We have to find this dog and fast," Pauline said. "Any idea where it might be?"

Jane shook her head. "I wouldn't have needed you if I did, would I?"

"Did you notice anyone in the street around your apartment that day?"

Jane shook her head.

"Think, Jane," Pauline begged. "The person who took the dog knew it was there and you were out. They must have been watching."

"I don't know," Jane cried. "I don't study the street when I'm at home or when I leave the house. I don't live where burglars are hanging around waiting for folks to leave."

"Do your neighbors have garages or park on the street?"

"Both."

"Was there a car on the street you didn't recognize?" Pauline asked. "Whoever did this didn't walk away with a dog under his arm."

"How should I know? Cars are just cars to me."

"Your neighbors, did they notice anything? Hear anything?"

"They were out too," Jane said. "At the same party actually."

"How did the kidnapper know to phone your friend Wendy?" Pauline wondered.

"Mimi has a tag with the phone number on it," Jane said. "It's really cute, a pink bow to match the one in her hair."

Pauline shook her head. What a mess. Without something to go on, there was no hope of finding the dognapper. Her best hope was to get Jane away to safety before her whereabouts was discovered.

"Who knew the dog was staying with you?" she asked.

"I wish you'd stop saying 'the dog' like that. Mimi is Wendy's baby and she's adorable. Better than any squalling brat would be, anyhow."

"I don't care, Jane. It's a dog. Who knew?"

"I might have mentioned it at the salon that day," Jane said, fidgeting uncomfortably. "I can't really remember."

Pauline groaned inwardly. Jane said she couldn't remember, but her refusal to meet Pauline's gaze said exactly the opposite.

"Who was in your salon that day, in case you did just mention it?"

Jane grabbed her bag and began burrowing among its contents. "Hah! Here it is. My appointment book."

She opened it to the page and said, "There was Mrs. Gormley's 'Hester' in the morning and Mrs. Delaval's 'Sam' in the afternoon."

"You know these people well?"

"Well, enough," Jane said, defensively. "Sadie Gormley's husband is a city councilor. They say he'll be mayor someday and Lance Delaval, Hannah's husband, is an impresario. He manages all the big club acts for the north of England. They're both friends of Tosh and Wendy."

Pauline sighed. "But do you *know* them?"

"As well as you can know clients," Jane said. "They don't steal dogs, if that's what you mean."

"But if you'd told them about Wendy's dog, might they have told someone else? Someone less honest than themselves, for example?" Really, this was like pulling teeth, Pauline thought.

"They might have," Jane said. "How can I know something like that?"

"If you knew these women well, you might have been able to say what they'd do," Pauline said. "I'm just casting around for something to explain how you take a dog and the next evening it's stolen when so few people knew you had it."

"My neighbors below knew," Jane said. "They were there when I came home with her."

"What sort of people are they?"

"He's a bass player with the *Shades of Blue*, soon to be a star, and Cyn's a model," Jane said.

"So, in the same world you all inhabit," Pauline said thoughtfully. "How successful are they really? Might they need money?"

"Everybody needs more money, Pauline," Jane said. "Even ordinary people like you need more money, though I can't see what you spend it on." Jane's gaze ran down Pauline from her hair to her feet with an expression of amused horror.

Pauline ignored the jibe and said, recapping the information, "We have two women and a couple down below who might have alerted the dognappers. There's also the possibility that your friend Tosh took the dog. Maybe he hated it and getting rid of it while she was with you would keep him in his wife's good books."

"That's crazy, Pauline," Jane said. "He loves Wendy and Wendy loves Mimi. He wouldn't hurt either of them."

Pauline frowned. Her instincts were all against this and Jane's casual description of the circumstances and people involved revolted her more than she thought possible. Yet, Freda was right. You supported your family, and this was a duty she could perform so she must. She considered explaining to Jane all the wrongness in Jane's friends, in her whole way of life, but knew it would be to no avail. Jane wouldn't understand.

"What we need is Inspector Ramsay's access to the police files," Pauline said, accepting her fate.

"Then phone him."

"He's retired," Pauline said. "He was invalided out. We can't hope for help from there."

"He could probably ask an old colleague," Jane said.

"That would be wrong," Pauline replied. "Wrong for Inspector Ramsay to ask and for his ex-colleague to provide the information."

Jane rolled her eyes. "You really are naïve, Pauline. For someone who thinks she's climbing the greasy corporate ladder, you haven't a clue. That's how it's done. You do favors for others, and you call in favors when you need them."

Pauline nodded. "You're right. I just don't agree with it. Nevertheless, I'll telephone him now and see what he can do."

She dialed the number she still had in her diary, but the phone rang and rang until she gave up. "He's out," she said to Jane, "I'll ring him again in the morning."

"We should interview Wendy," Jane said. "You might get something I've missed."

"We will, soon," Pauline agreed. "You said Mimi is Wendy's baby. Is she really that fond of it? She couldn't just buy another dog? After all, she was happy to leave Mimi in your care for a weekend."

"That cost her a lot of emotional stress, believe me," Jane said. "You've no idea. In the end, she trusted me and now look at how it turned out."

Pauline frowned in concentration. "And Tosh loves Wendy so much he'd hurt you to rescue a dog he doesn't much care for?"

Jane shrugged. "I guess," she said. "He's mad about her, always buying her expensive gifts, jewelry and furs. He says she's his queen and she should look like a queen."

"Has she a lover? Or does he suspect she has a lover? Is that why he's buying her gifts? To keep her with him?"

Jane laughed. "I'm sure she doesn't have a lover, no one would be mad enough to do that. Still, I see what you're driving at. He does act insecure, now that I think about it." She paused, thinking hard. "Wendy is worried about something too," she added.

"Worried?"

Jane nodded. "I don't know if worried is the right word but something's bothering her."

"Maybe she was frightened your pal Tosh was planning on doing something nasty to her when they were away."

Jane shook her head. "No, it was after that. Anyway, he's over-the-top in love with her, I'm sure of that. I think it may be his only redeeming feature." She paused, then added, "Still, if he did suspect her of infidelity..." She left the rest unsaid.

"In your world of people jumping in and out of each other's beds, could Wendy have slipped up? Or done something innocent that might make Tosh believe she'd betrayed him?"

Jane shuddered. "The problem for a queen is that simple

human infidelity becomes treason to the king." Her eyes caught Pauline's and held.

Pauline nodded. "Exactly so," she said quietly. "However, she's still around so it might not be that serious."

Jane frowned. "You never know with Wendy. Like I said, she's out of her head from morning to Christmas most days. She's either alone in the house or she's escorted by her driver. I know that gets her down. Maybe that's all it was."

10

RAMSAY CALLS IN SUPPORT

Wandering the few streets of Clifton and the footpaths that led out between the fields, Ramsay waited for the world to wake up and begin the day. He considered his avenues of inquiry while Bracken considered the local dogs and wildlife based on the scents they left behind. Neither was closer to forming a coherent strategy by the time they returned to the bed & breakfast where they were staying.

"I'll call my old colleague Inspector Morrison," Ramsay told Bracken, who nodded in agreement. "Maybe, I can learn of any other expensive pets gone missing."

Inspector Morrison was reluctant to help at first, he and Ramsay had never been close, but he did owe Ramsay for his first step on the ladder all those years ago and agreed to ask around in police circles for similar crimes or an officer in Manchester who could be approached. Ramsay wished there was a place where police officers throughout the land could quickly learn what crimes were being committed across the whole country, but he couldn't see how that would work. Even if a library was built big enough, who could sort and recover the information in a timely manner?

"Oh," Ramsay said, as he was about to hang up, "one more thing. You know about cars. What car would look like an Austin Cambridge but be bigger and flashier?"

Morrison answered immediately, "An Austin Westminster. You should know that."

Ramsay snorted. "I don't even know which of them out there is a Cambridge," he said. "So long as the damn thing goes, I don't need to know more."

"What are you driving now?"

"The same I always have, a Ford Popular," Ramsay said. "And I struggle to find it if I park where there are lots of other cars."

Morrison laughed. "Aye, I remember. Why the interest in this one?"

"A witness saw a car like I just described," Ramsay said. "He didn't know what it was either."

"They're expensive. They're for the metropolitan crowd rather than the ordinary man."

"That's good information," Ramsay said. "Why would one be parked outside a residential home in an out-of-the-way Lancashire village?"

"The owner's car?" Morrison suggested.

"Could be, thanks. Let me know as soon as you can about pet thefts, particularly here in the north-west," Ramsay reminded him before hanging up the phone. Who could tell him what the owner of the residential home drove? This is where Miss Riddell was so valuable. She could talk to people without seeming to be questioning them. It was going to be years before he got the 'police' out of his interview technique. He knew she now lived near Manchester but wondered exactly where she was.

"Bracken," Ramsay said. "We're going back to the residential home. Maybe today's shift will tell us something new, and at least we can find out if that car belongs to the owner of the home."

Bracken grinned. Ramsay knew his words were meaningless to Bracken, but he was sure the dog sensed it meant they were going out and that was always good.

"I'M SORRY, MR. RAMSAY," the nurse who answered the door said, "I wasn't at work that day so I can't help you." She paused as she stepped outside and pulled the door closed behind her before saying, "Though I must say, it doesn't surprise me the cat's gone. It was very disruptive."

"You think someone may have harmed her?"

"No, not that. Only, I think a lot of people would have held the door open to let her out, or even a window. She was always trying to escape. I think it was only a matter of time."

"I see. Did you hear the owner received a ransom note?"

"I did and I'm surprised. Knowing that cat, I'd imagine the thieves would pay the owner to take it back," the nurse said.

Ramsay laughed. "What did it do that was so bad?"

"It had its favorites and if you weren't one of them and tried to touch it, you got your hand clawed. I had a nasty cut for days just trying to get it back into Adie's room. I wasn't the only one. She really hated old Mr. Aymes. She'd hiss and arch her back if he just entered a room."

"That makes my job easier," Ramsay said. "I should look for someone whose hands and face are covered in plasters."

"You could do worse," the nurse agreed.

"Do you know anyone who drives an Austin Westminster?" Ramsay asked.

She shook her head. "Nay, but I don't know one car from another. John, our gardener, would know. He likes cars."

Ramsay thanked her, and following her direction, went round to the back of the building to find John. John, however, said no one in Clifton had a Westminster, though he thought he'd seen one parked outside at evening visiting times, but he didn't know who it belonged to.

"Does the owner, or anyone around here, have a bigger car, not your ordinary motor?" Ramsay ventured.

John shook his head. "Locally, there's a couple of Jaguars and a Bentley, that's it."

"They couldn't be mistaken for a Westminster, could they?"

John laughed. "Not by anyone with eyes, no."

Ramsay thanked him and returned to his B&B by a circuitous route that gave Bracken the time to burn off some energy by straining at the leash in the meadows where wary sheep watched them pass.

"We need to know which visitor owns that Westminster, Bracken," Ramsay said, thinking out loud as he surveyed high hills to the north and east. His few ventures into Northumberland's hill country had finally whetted his appetite for more and he longed to climb these new ones too, especially those he could see that had towers on the top.

11

PAULINE AND RAMSAY TOGETHER AGAIN

Pauline's attempts to reach Ramsay throughout the day were met with the sound of his phone ringing and she was beginning to lose hope when suddenly it was answered.

"Inspector?" she began.

"Nay, lass. I'm his neighbor just looking in to see everything's all right in his house."

"Oh," Pauline said. "Is Inspector Ramsay on holiday?"

"That's right," the woman replied. "He's down Manchester way somewhere, he said."

"You don't remember where?"

"Well, that's the funny thing," the woman replied. "He said Clifton but that's just up the road from here and nowhere near Manchester. I may have misheard, of course, I often do, but it was something like that."

Pauline thanked her, left her phone number in case Ramsay returned, and hung up. She ran down to her car and returned a few moments later with her copy of the *Manchester A-Z*.

"What are you looking for?" Jane asked, flicking through the latest Vogue.

"Is there a Clifton near Manchester, or a place that sounds like Clifton?"

Jane shrugged. "I've never heard of it."

"Ah ha!" Pauline cried, her finger running down the A-Z's index. "Got it. Come on, we're going for a drive."

"All right," Jane said, "but we go to my apartment first. I must get some things."

Pauline considered a flat 'no' but decided Jane had been away long enough for any observers to have given up and it was Sunday morning, a time the criminal classes generally spent in bed, in her mind.

"Very well," she said, "but be quick. You run in, grab what you need and run out. I'll keep watch."

The roads were quiet, and they were soon at Jane's flat, which, like Pauline's, was in an old Victorian home in a leafy suburb. Pauline parked on a side street, out of sight of any watcher, but within fast walking distance of the front door. They walked quickly to the door. Jane opened it and ran up the stairs that rose from the hallway. Pauline carefully scanned the street from one end to the other. She couldn't see anyone. It seemed it wasn't only the criminal class who spent Sunday morning asleep. After a moment, she heard a cry from above and, fearing for Jane's safety, ran upstairs.

"Look," Jane said, pointing through the open door. "Now you see why I'm scared?"

Pauline peered through the door. Jane's apartment was wrecked. Large furniture was whole, but every furnishing and decorative piece was torn or broken. The floor was strewn with shards from broken picture frames and glassware. Lewd and vicious words were scrawled on the walls, though with what Pauline didn't like to imagine. Someone had gone to a lot of trouble to make the point that Jane's well-being was in danger, and they'd done so exceedingly well.

"Get what you came for and let's go," Pauline said, pulling herself together.

Jane ran into the bedroom, glass crunching under her shoes, but returned empty handed. "My clothes, my undies, everything slashed to pieces," she said, her voice quavering. "It's horrible. Go and see."

Pauline shook her head. "No. Lock up. We're leaving now."

They ran downstairs and back to the car. Pauline started the engine and drove away before they'd caught their breath. For the next twenty minutes, she watched her rear-view mirror nervously for anyone following. Only when they were on the road to Clifton, did she relax and start looking about.

"What are we looking for?" Jane asked. Now they'd left the city behind she'd recovered her composure.

"A pale blue Ford Popular," Pauline replied. "My good friend Chief Inspector Ramsay, though he's not an inspector anymore, is in the village somewhere. We're not likely to see him but his car will be parked in a hotel car park or on the drive of a B&B or on the street, perhaps."

"How big is this place?" Jane asked, looking dubiously at her sister.

"On the map, it's small. We won't know for sure until we get there."

Fortunately, Clifton *was* small. A park surrounding a large mansion occupied much of one side of the road and a small village the other. There was only one pale blue Ford, and it was on the driveway of a bed & breakfast called *Dunroaming*. Pauline parked on the street and knocked on the door.

"Mr. Ramsay is out with his dog," the owner said but offered them a seat and a cup of tea.

Looking out onto the street through the bay window, they saw Ramsay before their cups of tea were finished. A moment later, he entered the house, and was shown into the sitting room.

"Miss Riddell," he said, beaming. "What a pleasant surprise."

Bracken eyed Pauline and Jane warily, shrinking back behind Ramsay, not at all sure he approved of these strangers that his friend appeared to like.

Pauline shook Ramsay's hand heartily. "I'm glad to see you also, Inspector."

"I'm not an inspector now," he said, laughing. "It's not like the army where you carry your rank out into the wider world."

"I'm afraid I think of 'Inspector' as your first name," Pauline said, smiling. She bent down to pat Bracken who was pushing himself between them. "And who is this?"

"This is Bracken, my new assistant sleuth. He'll track criminals to their lair," Ramsay said, beaming affectionately at Bracken. "Say hello, Bracken."

Bracken sat and extended a paw, which Pauline shook.

"I've been teaching him that for a month now," Ramsay said. "I think that's the first time he got it right."

"This is my sister, Jane," Pauline said, straightening up.

"I'm very pleased to meet you," Ramsay said, crossing the floor to where Jane was seated. Jane shook his hand nervously, which puzzled Ramsay. "Maybe Bracken can make my day by following his training twice." He ushered the collie to sit before Jane.

"How do you do, Bracken," Jane said, holding out her hand.

Bracken looked at it, looked at Ramsay, then back to Jane. He didn't lift a paw. Ramsay sighed. "I suspect him greeting Miss Riddell was a fluke."

"It's funny," Jane said. "Dogs and I generally hit it off right away."

"Say hello, Bracken," Ramsay urged, stroking the dog's head. Bracken yawned and flopped down on the floor.

"Pauline thinks you might be able to help us," Jane said quickly, to distract from Bracken clearly not doing as he was asked.

Ramsay turned to Pauline who shook her head. "I was hoping to work up to asking you for a favor," she said. "Not blurt it out right away."

Ramsay laughed. "I didn't imagine you tracked me down just to say hallo," he said. "I'm afraid the old cynic in me guessed you had a motive for being here. What is it?"

"When I'm telling you," Pauline said, "don't be writing it off in your head. This sounds feeble but somebody is desperately serious about this."

"You've whetted my appetite, Miss Riddell. What is it?"

"It's a missing pet," Pauline said, "and before you laugh..." She stopped. Ramsay wasn't laughing, he was puzzled.

"What kind of pet?" Ramsay asked, inviting her to sit. He took a chair opposite as Pauline continued.

"A dog," Pauline said. "Let me explain." She briefly outlined what had happened and what they found at Jane's apartment only an hour ago.

"Is this dog valuable in some way?" Ramsay asked Jane.

Jane shook her head. "Only to the owner, Wendy," she said. "She dotes on it."

"The reason I ask," Ramsay said, "is I'm here looking at a petnapping too. Only in this case, it's a cat and it's worth a lot of money." He explained about Mittens.

"I've heard of Mittens," Jane said, ignoring the bemused gazes of the others. "Lance Delaval, the impresario I told you about, Pauline, handles their contract on the northern club circuit."

"Does he know your friend Tosh?" Ramsay asked, quickly.

"Everybody knows Tosh," Jane said slowly, as if talking to a child. "You can't get anywhere in this city if you don't know Tosh."

Pauline and Ramsay exchanged glances. "That's the most hopeful thing I've heard since I got here," Ramsay said.

"It is a connection," Pauline agreed. "But like Jane said, people who manage things in a city are sure to know each other so it isn't exactly a strong connection."

"You're probably right," Ramsay said. "What leads have you been following, Miss Riddell?"

"I've only just become involved, Inspector," Pauline said, "and I'm at work during the week. I was hoping you might know someone in the local police force who would point me in a possible right direction."

Ramsay nodded. "I've got my old sergeant, now Inspector, Morrison, researching. I hope he'll have a contact for me very soon."

"Is there any way he might have heard of these pet thefts?" Jane asked.

Ramsay shook his head. "It's unlikely. Each force keeps its own records so unless they've had something similar happen up in the north-east it won't be passed on. Murders would, but not missing pets."

"I can't believe this is a national ring of kidnappers,"

Pauline said thoughtfully. "I think it has to be here in Manchester with maybe the odd foray into Liverpool."

"I don't think the Beatles have any pets," Jane said. "I haven't heard of it anyway. If I had, I'd have been looking to open a salon there."

Pauline rolled her eyes and shook her head. "For now, we concentrate on Mimi and Mittens and leave the rest of the entertainment industry to look after itself."

"It's not just entertainment," Jane protested. "Liverpool has a big football club too."

Ramsay grinned at Pauline's pained expression and said, before Pauline could respond to her sister's off-topic remarks, "Your sister is right though, Jane. If we recover Mimi and Mittens, we'll have achieved what we were asked to do. We must keep our focus narrow."

"Of course," Jane said, unconcerned. "I'm just saying there could be more crimes in Liverpool and they may give us another trail to follow."

"And if we learn of such a crime, we will certainly consider the evidence it provides," Ramsay said, "be sure of it. Now, Miss Riddell, what had you planned to do if I hadn't been here?"

Pauline frowned. "I'm at work all day tomorrow," she said, "and I'll ask people there if they've heard of any of our potential suspects. Someone may know something. In the evening, I planned to visit the Better Business Bureau, the library, and newspaper offices. Mittens and Mimi may be being kept in pet shops, kennels, or similar places. With a list, I could start visiting the most likely."

"How is your new job, Miss Riddell? We launched straight into the cases, and I didn't have time to ask."

"I thought it was going well," Pauline replied, "but a report I was asked to do has started a war between the executives. I'm constantly being forced to defend my findings in their battles. I fear that at some point, they may choose to shoot the messenger rather than each other."

"You don't need this investigation right now, do you?" Ramsay asked sympathetically.

"I don't but family is family, and I must help Jane."

Ramsay nodded. Turning to Jane, he said, "I hate to ask but do you have a dislike of the police? You're very wary of me, I think."

Jane reddened and Pauline stepped in to briefly explain Jane's unfortunate choices in life and her brushes with the law since being a teenager, before closing with, "and now she has friends who are almost certainly working outside the law for much of their time."

Jane cried, "Pauline has put the worst possible interpretation on everything. I'm wary because I don't know you and I've had bad experiences with the police. Now, you know."

"I see," Ramsay said, chuckling. "Then I'll try not to make things worse."

Pauline smiled. "And what will *you* do next to find Mittens, Inspector?"

"Now I know the names of some potential suspects," Ramsay said, "I'm going to press Morrison to find me a local man who can get me an introduction."

"You won't get an introduction to Tosh," Jane said gloomily. "He doesn't like coppers."

"He sounds like the sort of person whose experience of us has also been colored by being close to so many criminal people and endeavors."

"You can't call the city councilors criminals," Jane protested.

Ramsay laughed and turned to Pauline. "Where can I reach you when I have information from Morrison?"

Pauline wrote out her phone number on a page in her notebook and handed it over. "You can phone at any time," she said. "Jane will be home. She's hiding out in my flat." She gave Jane a stony stare to drive home the point.

"Have you a photo of Mimi?" Ramsay asked.

"We do," Jane said, diving into her bag. "I have all my clients' photos."

"Here's a leaflet I'm handing out around the neighborhood this afternoon and tomorrow," Ramsay said. He handed over two pages, one to Pauline and one to Jane with a black and white photo of Mittens at the top and contact details below. "As you see, there's a reward, if you find her."

Jane studied the leaflet for a moment, then said, "I wonder why Tosh hasn't thought of this?'

"Probably because he doesn't want anyone phoning him," Pauline said. "Anyway, he doesn't sound like the sort of man who would react well to a stranger turning up at his house with the missing dog."

"No, he wouldn't," Jane agreed. "He has a bit of a temper, and he doesn't trust many people."

"I can see why you so enjoy being around his wife," Pauline said drily.

"Oh, yes," Jane said, her expression brightening at once. "You wouldn't understand but they know how to live life.'

"Being afraid for your *own* life must, I imagine, make sharing *their* life more exciting than everyday existence."

Jane flushed red. "You can sneer, but it does. Life must be lived on the edge, or it isn't life."

Pauline shook her head at such lunacy. "We should leave you to get on, Inspector. While we follow our leads, such as they are."

Jane walked quickly ahead of Pauline and Ramsay and

was soon at the car, which allowed Ramsay to observe, "Your sister is even more fearless than you are."

"She's not fearless," Pauline said bitterly. "She's foolhardy and she's been that way since a child. Our parents indulged her because she was the baby, and this is how it turned out."

"She seems to be doing well in life, despite her unfortunate character traits," Ramsay pointed out, "so she can't be so very bad."

"We called her Calamity Jane when we were young," Pauline said hotly. "She was always having to be rescued from one unfortunate incident after another. She never learned because we all shared the cost, and she never did."

"Might be useful for the more daring parts of the investigation," Ramsay said, grinning.

"It's pet stealing, Inspector, not Russian spies or the Italian Mafia. We don't need daring to solve this."

Ramsay laughed. "I'm sure you're right, Miss Riddell. Now, you'd better go before your sister decides she's tired of waiting and breaks into your car."

Pauline followed his gaze and saw he was right. Jane was examining the doors with a look of criminal intent on her face.

"I'm coming, Jane," Pauline cried, hurrying back to her car all too aware how impetuous Jane could be. Breaking and entering her sister's car wouldn't seem in the least like wrongdoing to Jane and she'd do it if she saw a way.

As they drove away, Jane sighed and shook her head in a meaningful way.

"What?" Pauline asked.

"Your Inspector Ramsay," Jane said. "I was expecting a more impressive character. He looked like the knitted jumper, pipe, and slippers-by-the-fire sort of man to me."

"He's in his fifties, Jane, and invalided out of the force."

"Still, you must admit, he's no Gregory Peck. What do you see in him?"

"I see a decent man who has helped me when I needed it when no one else would have done," Pauline said, angry at having her friend described so cuttingly.

"Maybe, but no sex appeal at all," Jane said, laughing. "He wouldn't even be chosen as the lead in his own life story."

"Life isn't the entertainment industry, Jane."

"If he lost some weight and got some sunshine," Jane said thoughtfully, "I suppose, I could see what you see in him."

"Jane, I do not view Inspector Ramsay as a future husband," Pauline began.

"Understandably," Jane interjected.

Pauline bit her lip and said nothing more, which didn't slow Jane's commentary.

"He's middle-aged, balding, and defeated by life. You could do so much better if only you'd make some effort, Pauline. You aren't so old. Let me buy you some clothes and show you how to do makeup, you could get someone your own age."

"I thought I was the conventional one and you the woman forging her own modern life," Pauline said, laughing. "You sound like an old-fashioned matchmaker."

Jane chuckled. "Well, my offer is there when you're ready for it. Stephen died a long time ago. Move on."

Pauline ground her teeth but again said nothing.

12

RAMSAY GETS A LEAD

When the two women had gone, Ramsay set out to phone Morrison again. Now he had names of people who likely would show up in police records, he had a better chance of getting useful information than with inquiries concerning missing pets. He and Bracken walked quickly down the street to the local telephone box and called Morrison's home.

Morrison was in, Sunday afternoons being a dead time in the week where nothing was open and few entertainments available.

"You know, sir, this is frowned upon," Morrison said, when Ramsay had finished speaking.

"Frowned upon, yes," Ramsay said, "but I'm not a regular member of the public and I'm not a private investigator so I'm sure people will understand. What's happening here may be serious – if serious people are involved."

"But are they involved?" Morrison asked. "You have a connection between people but not to the missing pets, at least not criminally."

"It is odd, though," Ramsay said. "A city of a million people, two pets being held for ransom and one name with links to both of them."

Morrison sighed loudly enough for Ramsay to understand his request was a great imposition but finally said, "I'll let you know as soon as I can, but I'm not promising anything."

Ramsay thanked him and rang off. Exiting the telephone box, Ramsay said, "Bracken, we'll begin our leaflet campaign right now."

Bracken's expression was wary, like a dog who thought he was being tricked into sitting in a room on a fine day. However, once he realized they were going door to door, with all the exciting smells that entailed, his expression cheered up. It grew even happier when people in their gardens stroked and patted him after reading the leaflets they were given.

At one of the last houses Ramsay reached, Bracken found a friend. A spaniel puppy who wanted to play while Ramsay and the homeowner talked.

"Is it safe to let Bracken off the leash?" Ramsay asked.

"It is," the man replied. "I puppy-proofed the fence and gates when I got Charlie."

"He's a King Charles spaniel then," Ramsay said, stooping to unclip Bracken.

"You must be a detective," the man laughed. "He is." He paused before continuing, "I was up that way, by the residential home, taking Charlie for his walk."

Ramsay's ears perked up at this, like Bracken when he smelled a rabbit nearby. "Did you see anything suspicious?"

"Not suspicious but I did see a car like you mention in your leaflet."

"You wouldn't remember the number, I suppose," Ramsay said.

"No but it was a Manchester registration, NB, same as my own car, which is why I noticed. It may have been ANB and," he thought for a moment, "there may have been a nine in the number."

"Thanks," Ramsay said. "That will give me something to work on. You didn't see the driver?"

"It was dusk," the man said, "and with all the trees, it's quite dark in that lane when the sun's down but I think there were two people in the car. Both men."

"That might make sense," Ramsay mused. "One to drive and one to hold the cat."

"I hope you catch them," the man said. "I wouldn't want to be without Charlie. I've only had him a month and he's given me a new lease on life. The thought of him being stolen makes my blood run cold."

"I'll do my best," Ramsay said, wishing the man farewell. As they walked Ramsay said to Bracken, "We just might find the owner of that car, if I can find a friendly supporter in the Manchester police." He paused and then added, "And Miss Riddell's sister may have an idea too, if we ask."

His call, when he made it, after waiting long enough for Pauline and Jane to return home, didn't help. Jane didn't know anyone with car number plates he described.

"I don't know anyone's car plates," she said. "Do you?"

"I do, actually," Ramsay said, grinning, "but I realize noticing car license plates is very much a police trait and not the public's."

"We have some news," Jane said. "You'll want to hear it."

"Then tell me."

Jane's words tripped over themselves as she launched into a fast-paced replay of a telephone conversation she'd just had with a friend.

Ramsay laughed. "Slow down," he cried. "Take a deep breath and explain slowly."

"I can't," Jane said. "Pauline can. She's as wooden as you'd like."

Ramsay waited as the phone was handed over and then said, "Well?"

"Jane phoned one of her safer friends. During the conversation, she learned the kidnappers have been in touch again, by phone to Wendy this time, and they're demanding another thousand and they want it sooner," Pauline said. "I fear we won't solve this before they run out of patience and Jane really will have to flee the country for safety. And it seems this man, Tosh, is convinced she's behind it, even more so now Jane has gone into hiding."

"I see why Jane is nervous," Ramsay said. "Did you see the car I asked Jane about?"

"I've only just joined this lost cause of a case," Pauline protested. She paused. "Oh, you mean in the street outside Jane's flat when we found it damaged?"

"I thought it a possibility," Ramsay said.

"I didn't but if it had been, I'm sure it would have followed us so I think we can assume it wasn't."

"I suppose you're right," Ramsay said. "Well, be sure to watch the street outside your apartment for anything remotely similar."

"I will," Pauline said. "How soon might your old colleague Morrison phone back? I don't think we have long before the kidnappers choose to make an example of someone's pet."

"He can't even start looking until he goes into work

tomorrow and you can be sure there'll be a pile of work waiting in his in-tray, so I don't hold out much hope for a quick response."

"Then my only remaining hope is they have another pet we don't know of and that's the one they mutilate. I'm sure they'll leave Mimi safe for as long as they can. No matter how hardened they are as criminals, I'm sure they know what will happen to them if they hurt that dog and they're caught by Tosh."

"It would be no more than they deserve," Ramsay said. "Now I have Bracken, I understand how pet owners feel."

"Have you any ideas how to proceed, Inspector?" Pauline asked. "I don't. My talking to Mimi's owner risks giving Jane's location away and even if I do talk to her, she likely won't know anything."

"She may recognize the car," Ramsay said. "I'm going to phone Magic Mal and see if he does and also, if he's received an increased ransom demand."

Pauline wished him luck and they ended the call. Ramsay found Magic Mal's card in his wallet and dialed the number.

"We'll have to be quick," he told Mal, when Mal picked up his phone. "I'm running out of coins." He quickly asked about the car and ransom demands and got a negative answer to both questions, which was a disappointment. Some movement, even a negative one like a renewed demand, would have been welcome. As it was, he had little enough news to go on.

The renewed and increased ransom demand worried Ramsay. He had no experience with kidnapping, it was a crime hardly known in his part of the world, but it seemed to him to suggest the kidnappers were growing desperate.

Either the dog was unwell, or they were finding it hard to manage; perhaps it was refusing to eat. Whatever the reason, it didn't bode well for Miss Riddell's sister, Jane. Emigration under a new name was probably the best option if this went as badly as he now feared it might.

13

PAULINE ALSO GETS A LEAD

PAULINE, however, was much more fortunate than Ramsay with her phone call. Summoning her courage, she'd phoned Wendy who was at home.

After Pauline had explained that she was Jane's sister and that she was looking for Mimi to help Jane, Wendy interjected, "Jane told me about you. She says you're good at solving puzzles."

"I've had some success," Pauline said, "and I'm not the police. Often that helps to get information people wouldn't share with the authorities."

"You're not working with the police now, are you?"

"Definitely not," Pauline replied. "It's strictly private and personal."

"All right," Wendy said. "Why are you phoning me?"

Pauline explained about the car and Wendy said she recognized the car or thought she did.

"You're not sure?" Pauline asked.

"I don't know much about cars," Wendy said, "but it sounds like one Brian Brereton drives."

"What can you tell me about him?" Pauline asked.

"He's young, twenties, cocky, and useless," Wendy said. "He comes here to meet Tosh sometimes. Why? Has he got Mimi?"

"It was just a car seen nearby that people didn't recognize," Pauline said, being careful not to say nearby *where*. "Even if it was his car, it may have had nothing to do with Mimi's disappearance," She added hastily, suddenly realizing if Wendy told her husband, Brian Brereton could be in desperate trouble without having any idea what he was accused of.

"I won't tell Tosh if you tell me he had nothing to do with it," Wendy said.

"Then you have to give me time to speak to Brereton," Pauline said. The stakes in this investigation kept getting raised and she was no gambler.

"Be quick," Wendy replied. "I have my own reasons for wanting to talk to him."

"Have you phoned him?"

"I have but he doesn't pick up," Wendy said.

"He must be away," Pauline replied. "Any idea where?" There was an edge to Wendy's voice Pauline didn't like.

"No, but if you see him, tell him I want to talk to him," Wendy said. Again, her voice was chilling.

"I will," Pauline said brightly, "and perhaps you'll do the same if you see him first." She hung up the phone and breathed a deep sigh of relief. She'd faced some unpleasant people in her years of sleuthing but none of them had voices with quite that degree of iciness.

"Jane," Pauline said, turning to her sister who'd been flicking through yet another fashion magazine during the phone call, "do you know this man, Brian Brereton?"

Jane nodded. "A bit," she said. "Why?"

Pauline sensed Jane wasn't being entirely honest.

"Because Wendy says the car might belong to him. Yet, you didn't recognize it."

"I told you," Jane said, turning pink, "I don't know cars."

"Do you *know* him," Pauline said meaningfully.

"We've dated occasionally," Jane replied, now blushing.

"You mean you've been in his car, and he's been to your flat?"

"Yes," Jane replied. "You think he might have taken Mimi?"

"Jane," Pauline said. "This isn't difficult. Mimi was stolen by someone who knew you had the dog, knew where you lived, knew they could walk into and out of your place anytime. You told me you couldn't think of anyone who might do such a thing."

"My friends aren't bad people," Jane protested.

"So far as I've learned from you in the past days," Pauline said, "that's exactly what they are."

"Well, not to each other," Jane replied. "Brian wouldn't hurt Wendy and Tosh, they're friends."

Pauline shook her head in disbelief at such naiveté. "You need to phone him right now and get him to convince you he's not who we're looking for. If Wendy loses patience and decides to have Tosh investigate, Brian could end up in a concrete foundation."

Pauline's words, and the agitated way she said them, convinced Jane who quickly found Brian's phone number from her diary and dialed. There was no answer.

Jane replaced the handset and said, "He'll be clubbing somewhere."

"On a Sunday night?"

"This is the big city, Pauline. Here the world doesn't stop on Sundays."

Pauline didn't doubt it. They were a godless lot, Jane's

friends. "Call him again later," Pauline said, "and again tomorrow morning, but don't give him a clue as to where you're staying or who with. I don't want my place to look like yours does now."

"He likely won't be home until the early hours," Jane said, "and he won't welcome an early morning call."

"You have to make him understand his life may depend on Wendy being convinced he's not holding her dog," Pauline said. "That may make him welcome your early morning call."

"It'll make him think I shopped him," Jane cried, growing alarmed. "How am I going to even talk about this without him blaming me? I'll have him after me as well as Tosh."

"I don't know," Pauline said, "but we've started this rolling and it will end badly if we can't get him to prove it isn't him. I think alerting Wendy to Brereton's car has made her suspicious. She wants to talk to him herself now."

Jane shook her head. "No! Wendy has had a schoolgirl crush on Brian for years. We laugh about it sometimes. She just wants to hear his voice and imagine he's whispering sweet nothings in her ear."

"What kind of drugs is she on?" Pauline cried. "She's playing with fire."

"Just the prescription ones," Jane said. "You know, Librium, Valium, that sort of thing. Tosh would go mental if he found illegal drugs in the house."

Pauline frowned. "Her voice didn't sound like she was wanting to talk sweet nothings, Jane," Pauline said. "Asking about that car may have been a serious mistake."

"I thought you were good at this kind of thing, Pauline," Jane cried. "You've made it worse, much worse."

"And now we have to make it better," Pauline said. "Let

me speak to him, instead. I thought if you were close, it may be better from you. I see now we need to keep you well out of it."

Jane handed Pauline her diary and Pauline noted the number. "I'll set an even earlier alarm for the morning."

THE PHONE RANG AND RANG. In Pauline's imagination Brian had placed it under a cushion, it sounded so distant and muffled. She let it ring until she got the 'no answer' message and hung up. She ate breakfast and prepared herself for work before calling again.

Again, it rang on and on and she was about to hang up when a woman's voice said, dreamily, "Yes?"

"I'd like to speak to Brian," Pauline said.

The woman giggled. "He's busy," she said.

"Tell him it's urgent. He could be in danger."

There was a muffled conversation and a man's voice said, "Who is this?"

"You don't know me," Pauline replied, "but I'm looking into the disappearance of Wendy McIntosh's dog. A car like yours was seen nearby and I want to eliminate your car from my enquiries." She rather liked the official sound of that.

"What are you talking about? What car? What dog?"

Pauline's heart sank, he seemed genuinely puzzled. "A car like your Austin Westminster was seen near where another pet was snatched."

"There are lots of Austin Westminsters," he replied.

"There aren't that many with local license plates," Pauline said.

"I don't know why you're calling me about this," he said angrily. "Are you the police?"

"No, but they will know about it soon and Wendy

already does," Pauline said, growing agitated. "So, tell me honestly where you and your car were on these two dates." She read them out to him and waited.

"How can I remember things like that off the top of my head at this time of the morning?" He was yelling now. The mention of Wendy had finally filtered through.

"Get yourself out of bed, do some thinking and I'll phone again at noon," Pauline said. "It isn't just me you have to convince, remember that." She hung up and breathed a huge sigh. All her limbs were trembling. She couldn't begin to imagine how Brian Brereton felt.

14

RAMSAY FINDS THE LINK

Ramsay had more success with his latest phone call. Morrison was in his office. With something specific like a partial license plate to work with, he said he'd would phone Manchester police right away.

"Thanks," Ramsay said. "And get me a contact too while you're on, will you. Oh, and any word on that impresario, Delaval, I asked about?"

"He's clean with regards criminal records," Morrison replied. "Though he's known to be a drug user, apparently. He's never been arrested."

"Nothing about him being in debt or other signs of going off the rails?"

"Not that's reached police records," Morrison replied. "But you know how it is; by the time it reaches us he'd be a long way down the slippery slope. You need a muck-raking journalist for his present situation. Where's that young Poppy that used to hang around Miss Riddell?"

"She's in London these days, I understand," Ramsay replied. "Thanks for this. Get me the other stuff quick as you can."

Morrison said he'd do his best and Ramsay ended the call.

"Now," he said to Bracken waiting patiently at the door, "why don't we visit the place that car was? I can look for cigarette ends or other rubbish they may have left behind while you see if you can pick up a scent."

As all this was being said, Ramsay was putting on a jacket and hat and clipping the leash to Bracken's collar. Bracken was happy to do anything asked of him. Even finding week old scents along well traveled country lanes seemed possible.

Though he'd secretly held out little hope of finding anything after such a period, Ramsay was delighted to find two expensive cigarette ends with filters. The brand was still visible on them, Peter Stuyvesant. He never placed bets, but he would happily bet no local man bought or smoked these. He wrapped each carefully in his handkerchief and put the bundle in his pocket.

"What have you found, Bracken?" he asked. Bracken was sniffing at the verge where the passenger side door of the car would have been if they were waiting ready for someone to deliver Mittens from the residential home. Bracken followed the scent back along the lane before coming to a halt, unable to decide which way next.

Ramsay walked to where Bracken had first found a scent. The grass was crushed by footprints facing the ditch and hedge across it. He laughed. The passenger had stepped outside to relieve himself and the scent had lingered long enough for Bracken to find it. Then, he reasoned, the scent Bracken had followed down the lane toward the residential home may have been the person delivering the cat. Would Bracken recognize the person today if they re-visited the home? He could only try.

Ramsay rang the bell and waited. The same nurse as before opened the door.

"Hello again," she said. "Are you here to see Adie?"

"I am, if she's ready for visitors," Ramsay said, trying to maintain eye contact while also seeing if Bracken was reacting strangely to the woman. He wasn't and she let them in. Bracken trotted past her without any sign of recognition.

When Ramsay and Adie were alone, he asked if there was anyone on the home staff she thought might be open to taking Mittens away for money.

"There's a janitor I don't like," she said, "but that doesn't mean he would steal a cat."

"Is he here today?"

"I haven't seen him, but he should be," Adie said. "Why?"

"I'm still looking to talk to anyone who might know something," Ramsay said. "I don't believe I spoke to him last time I was here."

"He's somewhere about," Adie said. "Ask the nurse, she'll find him for you."

"I will, on my way out," Ramsay said. "Now, let us talk some more about what happened in the days leading up to Mittens' disappearance."

"I've told you all I know," Adie said peevishly. "It's no good to keep asking me questions."

"But you may remember something important, something you don't know is important, with the passing of time," Ramsay said. "You'd be surprised how often it happens."

"Well, it hasn't happened to me yet," Adie snapped.

"Then I should go and find the janitor," Ramsay said, smiling.

Outside Adie's room, he went in search of the nurse and

came upon what could only be the janitor. It wasn't just the coveralls the man was wearing, or the mop and bucket he was carrying, it was the way Bracken stiffened and sniffed.

"Hello," Ramsay said, catching the fellow's attention. "I was hoping to have a word. Have you a minute?"

"Not really, I'm busy," the janitor replied, moving away, eyeing the growling Bracken with distaste.

"It will really be only a minute," Ramsay said, following the man until the janitor stopped and faced him.

"Well?"

"I wondered if you saw Mittens the night she disappeared?" Ramsay asked.

He shook his head, then added, "Does somebody say so?"

"No," Ramsay said, quickly sensing the man's reluctance to speak. "I'm asking everyone if they saw the cat that night and I missed you when I was here last time."

"Well, I didn't," the janitor said, "so you can go now."

"Not even that afternoon or evening, wandering the corridors?"

"No! I said!" With that, the janitor turned away, hurrying off down a corridor.

Ramsay watched him go. If the man had admitted he stole Mittens, Ramsay thought, he couldn't have made himself look more guilty.

"Well, Bracken," Ramsay said, "what do you say?"

Bracken gave a low growl, and his expression said the man was a villain.

"I think we've learned everything there is to know here. Let's walk and think."

Their walk took them again along the lane where the car had parked, and Bracken immediately growled at the scent he'd found previously.

"You don't have to tell me," Ramsay said. "He even looks like a wrong 'un." It was true. The janitor was badly groomed, stubble on his chin, hair uncombed, his eyes shifty, darting everywhere but to Ramsay's face. "But, Bracken, as an investigator you'll learn not to judge a book by its cover. After all, we don't know if the man walks this way to and from home every day and that's why his scent is here. We must keep an open mind."

Bracken's expression said clearly he didn't judge by appearance and his information was never wrong.

"Nevertheless," Ramsay continued, "we need to speak to Miss Riddell. What she learns from this man Brereton may be all we need. This may be the simplest case to solve I've ever been on."

15

PAULINE FINDS IT'S NOT THAT SIMPLE

Pauline waited for Brereton to pick up the phone. When he did, his anger and fear were palpable even down the telephone line.

"Never mind all that," Pauline said to end his blustering denials of any involvement. "What proof have you?"

"I was with a woman on the first date you gave me. I can't tell you her name, she's married," he said. "On the second, I was in a club with hundreds of others. Someone there will remember."

Pauline sighed. "This woman has to come forward," she said. "And you must have been with some actual people at the club. One of them, preferably a respectable one, needs to come forward as well."

"It's not that simple," Brereton cried. "She'd be in danger of her life if it became known I was with her, and at the club I moved around. I didn't stay all night with the same people."

Pauline wanted to scream 'how do you people live this way?' but she bit her tongue and said, "Find a way to make them convince me, or your life is in danger too. Not from me but from your friend Tosh if Wendy loses patience."

"I'll try but..." further words failed him.

"You better try," Pauline said, "and quickly. I don't know Wendy but I'm sure she's frightened enough about her dog to demand her husband do something. If I don't have a convincing story to tell her today, she likely will, starting with you."

"I'll call you back soon," Brereton said.

"You have till five o'clock when I get home," Pauline said. "I'm not giving you my work number." She hung up just as the pips were sounding and the telephone was asking for more money.

She phoned Brereton shortly after arriving back at her apartment that evening. "Well?" she said brusquely, when he answered.

"She'll talk to you on the phone tonight. If I give her your number," Brereton said. "And I've one of the people I went to the club with who will vouch for me. He'll call tonight as well."

Pauline's blood seemed to freeze in her veins. How easy would it be for Brereton or either of these other people to get the address connected to her phone number? She didn't know but there was no other choice, so she read it out for him.

"Very well, have them phone me," she said. "I'll phone Wendy the moment I hear enough to be satisfied. If I don't, I'll call you and you'll have a head start on Tosh's thugs." His reply was a stream of obscenities that had her quickly hanging up the phone.

Her next phone call came from Inspector Ramsay while she and Jane were still eating their evening meal.

"I know how the cat got out of the residential home," he

said. "And I'm confident we can find that car to finish the trail."

Pauline explained about her talk with Wendy, and about Brereton potentially being the owner of the car.

"And has he satisfied you on the subject of his whereabouts those nights?' Ramsay asked.

"I'm waiting for his alibis to phone me," Pauline said. "It won't be entirely convincing, I'm sure, but it might be enough to hold Wendy off for a few days."

"You know," Ramsay said, "I would never have believed this if it had come across my desk at the station. Potential murders over kidnapped pets? It's incredible."

"They aren't just any pets though, are they," Pauline said. "There's money and fame attached to these two animals; they have value because of who owns them. That kind of worth always attracts greedy, unscrupulous people."

"Phone me when you've heard from these alibis," Ramsay said. "For my mind, I'm happy that the janitor took the cat and handed it to your man Brereton, and that's before I hear back about other possible car owners. I think this case is done. A cocky idiot saw a way of turning his rich contacts into a little gold mine and has screwed up big time."

"I said I'd give him enough warning to get away," Pauline cautioned.

"Don't say anything until he's told you where those animals are," Ramsay said. "Keep him dangling, make him sweat. He knows where they are, and we need them back. Make him see it's in his best interest as well."

"I'm not good at making people sweat, Inspector," Pauline said, "but I'll try."

"Harden your heart, Miss Riddell," Ramsay said. "Somebody could get killed or seriously hurt over this nonsense and you have a chance to stop all that. Your sister being one of the possible victims."

"Not to mention the pets," Pauline reminded him. "Somehow, I find their plight more concerning than the people's."

"Then focus on them but get an answer."

"I will," she said. She paused. "I think we should go to the police with what we have. I'm sure you're right about the people involved and the police would have a better chance of finding the pets than we have."

"When Morrison gets me a name, I will," Ramsay said. "I don't think simply walking into police headquarters and accusing people of crimes without any proof will get the local police to act. We need a contact who has been briefed ahead of time."

"Very well," Pauline said. "Now I just have to wait by the phone to speak to these alibis."

THE FIRST CALL came an hour later, when Pauline and Jane were losing hope. It was already growing late, and Wendy's patience could snap at any time.

"Who is this?" Pauline asked, when the woman started whispering that she could confirm Brereton's whereabouts on the night in question.

"I'm not telling you that," the woman whispered, "and I won't appear in court either. Only, Brian says you wanted to hear someone confirm his whereabouts. That's what I'm doing."

"But you could be anybody," Pauline protested, "his sister, even."

"He hasn't got a sister, leastways not as I know of," the woman whispered. "Anyhow, he was with me from early that evening until the early hours of the morning. My husband was away."

Pauline frowned but said, "Is there anything you can tell me that would give this story credence?"

"Like what?" the woman hissed. "Don't be stupid."

Pauline thanked her and she rang off.

"Well?" Jane demanded.

"A woman who won't give her name says Brian Brereton was with her the evening of Mimi's abduction and into the following morning." Pauline gave Jane a scrutinizing stare. "Her husband was away. Does that seem likely to you?"

Jane's face broke into a broad smile. "It sounds like Brian, yes."

"Then I'll take her word. Now to call Wendy with the news."

When told of Brereton's alibi, Wendy also thought it likely for she accepted Pauline's statement with an angry laugh, which startled Pauline. She'd imagined these people were happy to know of each other's infidelities. Perhaps normal human feelings sometimes got in the way, even for people like these.

"Tell Jane she must get away," Wendy said, after a moment. "The new ransom demand has made Tosh furious. He's out for blood and Jane is first in his sights. He's sure he can wring the truth out of her. Did you tell Brian I want to speak to him?"

"I did and I'll tell Jane to get out too," Pauline said. "Now, can you tell me who makes these demands and how? Is it by telephone or by a note?"

"It was a note, pushed through our letter box."

"May I see it?"

"Tosh has it. He said he's given it to the police."

"Who in the police?" Pauline asked. "Maybe I can talk to him and learn more about it."

"I don't know," Wendy said. "That's all he told me. There are several officers he works with. I don't think they would want to talk to you anyway. It's not official."

Pauline could believe it. "Is there a reason you want to talk to Mr. Brereton, Wendy? Maybe if I could explain what you wanted…" She let the sentence die away unfinished.

"It's personal," Wendy said. "Nothing to do with Mimi."

Not entirely convinced, Pauline wrapped up the call quickly and told Jane what Wendy had told her. "And I agree, Jane. You should go away for a week or two, at least until Inspector Ramsay and I have solved this case, which can't be long now. Brereton must be the receiver of the pets, even if he works through others, like the janitor, for the initial snatch."

"He couldn't have received Mittens if that married woman was telling the truth," Jane pointed out.

"We only have her word for what time their night of passion started," Pauline replied. "He could have driven straight to her house from dropping off Mittens. So, I repeat, you must go away for a while."

"I'm not going anywhere," Jane replied. "It's like being in a movie. I'm not missing a moment of this."

"In films," Pauline protested, "the hero and heroine always come out on top. This is real life, Jane, and in real life not all the cast live happily ever after."

Jane shook her head. "Not only am I not going anywhere. I'm going to start investigating on my own."

"Investigate what?" Pauline cried.

"Pet shops, kennels, pet salons: places where people put their pets when they go away from home. All places I'm familiar with and you aren't."

"If you're familiar with them, they're familiar with you," Pauline responded. "It isn't safe, someone will talk."

"They won't recognize me," Jane said. "I've bought hair dye, spectacles, and frumpy clothes. I'll look almost like you." She laughed and ran to the bathroom, returning with a bottle of auburn dye. "What do you think?"

"I'm only surprised it isn't bleach-blonde or redhead," Pauline said. She was less surprised Jane had ignored her about leaving the apartment. It had always been a forlorn hope Jane would comply.

"That would be no good," Jane said, seriously. "I've often been both. It had to be something dull, and you'll be amazed to learn they don't sell mousy hair colors. This was the closest I could find."

"I'm not in the least amazed," Pauline said rather crossly.

"You should see the suit I bought," Jane continued slyly. "You'll like it. If you do, I'll give it to you when this is all over."

"We aren't the same size," Pauline said dismissively. Jane's wind-ups were always tiresome, and even more so at a time like this.

Jane laughed. "Give me half an hour and tell me if you think I'll be recognized."

Thirty minutes later, Jane was indeed transformed. Not into an investigator, more a librarian, the sort who tut-tutted if you even whispered in her library. A dark brown tweed skirt and matching jacket over a fawn knitted sweater, covering a white lace blouse with the collar showing at the neck, all transformed Jane into, well, Pauline had to admit it, into a younger Pauline. With the round cheap glasses and auburn hair pulled back into a bun, even Jane's face looked different.

"They'll recognize your voice," Pauline said, and Jane

promptly began speaking with what, to Pauline, sounded like a passable Mancunian accent of the sort she was hearing every day at work.

"It's your life," Pauline said, shrugging. "I can't stop you if you want to throw it away."

"You're not the only one who can face life's dangers, Pauline," Jane said. "And it's my life, my case. I can't think why I brought you into it, to be honest. I thought you had some flair for investigating but I haven't seen any of that so far."

"Investigating is mainly searching and thinking, Jane. Not physical heroics, which I've no doubt you'd welcome."

Jane's smile grew even broader. "I would," she said. "Look." She drew out a long pin holding the beret style hat to her hair. "A nasty surprise for any attacker, don't you think?" It was easily six inches long and gleamed in the light.

Pauline shook her head but said nothing.

Triumphant, Jane said, "I'm starting in the morning with an out-of-town kennel I've heard is a bit dodgy."

"Take care, Jane. If they're a bit dodgy, they won't like you descending on them asking questions."

"I'm not going to. I'm going to be a rambler tomorrow. I'll borrow your binoculars, and satchel for sandwiches and flask. They won't even notice another sad old biddy out birdwatching."

16

CALAMITY JANE BEGINS INVESTIGATING

STEPPING down from the train on the wet suburban station that was nearest her first target, Jane wrinkled her nose in disgust. The rain was falling in a thin, almost mist-like fashion. Not hard, just steadily soaking. She fastened her raincoat and put on the clear plastic hood she'd brought with her. On her feet, she was wearing very unbecoming rubber boots more suited to a gardener, but they were all she could find in Pauline's limited clothes closet. One day, she would take Pauline shopping and buy her a new wardrobe.

The walk from the station and out into the fields behind the kennels left her cold and shivering. She wished she'd borrowed one of Pauline's thicker sweaters as well. Following a track up a hill with trees on the crest, Jane soon found a spot out of the sharp wind with a clear view down to the kennels below. Leaning against a tree, she fiddled with the binoculars until the kennels came into focus. She wasn't used to binoculars and was surprised to find how little she could see through them. Slowly, she swept them across the property, hoping for something that looked suspicious.

"Nobody will take dogs out in this rain," she said quietly to herself. She'd barely finished speaking when a man in a heavy raincoat stepped out of the house and made his way to the smaller buildings where the animals were kept. He made his way through a gate in the fenced off area in front of the building's door, closing the gate carefully behind him. At the building, he removed the lock on the door and opened it.

Jane wasn't surprised to find none of the animals inside rushing out. She wouldn't either, had she been one of them. The man disappeared inside the building and clearly began herding the animals out for they appeared, reluctantly, at the door. One by one, the dogs were pushed outside, where they clustered against the wall, sheltering from the weather. Jane studied each dog in turn, which was made easier by them not wanting to move, until she was sure that Mimi wasn't one of them. After fifteen minutes, the man stepped out from the building where he'd been sheltering from the rain, and the dogs shot back inside.

"Not exactly what the owners imagined would happen when they put their beloved pets in this place," Jane muttered. She continued her watch as the man left the fenced area and moved to the next small building where he went through the same routine. Mimi wasn't among the dogs pushed out into the rain this time either. The procedure was repeated on the third and last building with the same result and Jane was ready to quit when it came to her – Mimi might be so important, she was being kept separately from the others. Perhaps in the house.

The man returned to the house and Jane hoped he would soon re-appear with Mimi. He didn't and she grew increasingly cold and uncomfortable as she waited. She'd also noticed the only animals in the buildings were dogs. If other animals were being held here, it had to be in the house for there were no other buildings. She needed to see inside the house. Anyway, anything was better than standing in the cold, even with trees providing some shelter.

Her watch said eleven o'clock, which meant she'd been here more than an hour. Her mind and heart were in turmoil. She couldn't stay but knew creeping up to the windows of the house was a highly risky venture, particularly if the owners of this business were as crooked as everyone said they were.

Trying to look like a birdwatcher driven back to shelter by the weather, Jane moved slowly down the hill on the track that took her nearest to the kennels. The track took her around the garden of the house and along a side with no windows. Looking both ways and seeing no one, Jane pushed through the tall, unkempt hedge and into the garden. At the corner of the building, she ducked low and made her way to the first window, quickly peeking inside. A man and woman were sitting in armchairs in front of a fireplace where glowing coals looked so warming, Jane was tempted to ask for shelter. She ducked lower and crept under the window, past the door the man had used to visit the dogs, and on to the next window. Again, she peeked quickly inside. The room was empty but tidily furnished. A room to entertain visitors, she guessed.

She crept under this window too, though the room was empty, and made her way around the corner to the farther side of the house. This side had one window with frosted glass, so likely a lavatory, and one curtained that, when she peeked inside, proved to be a kitchen with an old-fashioned cast-iron hearth and oven, smartly blackened. At least the lady of the house managed her home well. The room had a small table and chairs and shelves of plates and pans, but no sign of any animals, expensive or otherwise.

Jane ended her inspection of the house by rounding the last corner and forcing her way through the hedge to the lane on which the house fronted. On this side, she could walk past the windows and look inside without any fear of detection. She was simply a curious passerby. However, her inspection of these rooms didn't add anything to what she'd already come to realize. The business may not treat its doggy clients well but judging by the view through its windows it wasn't harboring kidnapped pets. Disappointed, she returned to the station and a train back to Pauline's flat where she hung her wet clothes in front of the small two-bar electric fire and soaked herself in a hot bath.

PAULINE LET herself into her apartment to find Jane wrapped in a thick robe, towel on her head, in front of the electric fire, sipping what could only be a vodka cocktail.

"You've had a hard day, I see," Pauline said.

"I have," Jane replied, and told Pauline of her hour in the rain watching the suspect kennels.

"So, they didn't have Mimi," Pauline said, "and we don't know that Mittens is being held there either."

"She wasn't in a downstairs room but what about upstairs?" Jane said stubbornly.

"Jane," Pauline said, "this is the first place you've looked at. Don't jump to conclusions."

"We have to get inside," Jane replied, as if Pauline hadn't spoken.

"If we can provide evidence, the police will do that," Pauline said, "but you must look at the others before deciding this is the one."

"I'll have evidence by tomorrow night," Jane said.

"Jane, you are *not* to enter those premises," Pauline said. "If you're caught, you're trespassing at best, breaking and entering at worst. Don't do it. Look for evidence but from the outside."

"I thought you were forever breaking the law to get results," Jane said, shaking her head in disbelief at her sister's timidity.

"When the evidence is there, we can take risks," Pauline said. "We have no evidence yet."

NEXT MORNING, before she left for work, Pauline reminded Jane of what she'd said.

"I heard," Jane replied. "Get evidence, then we go in."

"That's not what I said," Pauline countered. "I said we or the police can go in when there's evidence, not that you see something you think is evidence and then barge right in. We don't do anything without alerting the police first."

"I'll be good," Jane said, following her sister to the door and closing it firmly behind Pauline. She watched from a window as Pauline drove off before dressing for her role as middle-aged birdwatcher and leaving the house.

The train once again dropped her off at the kennel. Today was sunny, unlike yesterday's visit, and she heard dogs outside. They weren't visible to her because the hedge was as tall as she was. Farther along, a gap in the hedge allowed her a glimpse into the yard where the dogs were playing. None looked like Mimi, and all looked like they needed her grooming services. When this was over, and they'd found the villains, she would persuade the owners of this kennel to promote her salon's services. It would increase her business and put some extra money in their pockets too.

Jane carried on until she'd reached the back of the property. Here the hedge was replaced by a wall with barbed wire running along the top. Not very welcoming but practical, she thought. Fortunately, another rough lane ran along the back of the property to what looked like a garage. Trying to look nonchalant, she walked alongside the wall, watching the dogs. The dogs, however, were interested in her and ran to the wall to greet her. Jane cursed under her breath. This attention was sure to arouse the kennel owners and she didn't want to explain why she was here.

In the moments she took to assemble a semi-sensible story about why she was where she was, it became clear the owners weren't coming out to see what the dogs were fussing over. She stopped and spoke to the dogs, who were jumping at the wall, hoping to be stroked, all the while watching the house. No one appeared at the windows or the door. Mimi wasn't here in the yard, but could she be in the house? And Mittens as well?

Jane said goodbye to the dogs and returned the way she'd come. She'd passed a gate in the hedge earlier that could allow her to get close enough to look in the windows. The gate was locked but low enough to be climbed over, using its support posts and the hedge for hand and footholds. Hitching up her heavy woolen skirt, Jane threw her leg over the gate and dropped inside the garden before making her way quickly to the nearest window. Fortunately, the pen where the dogs were kept was fenced on the house side and they couldn't come to greet her in person. Their welcoming barks, however, were enough to waken any sleeping kennel owner if they were inside.

She peered into the first window. Unlike yesterday, lace curtains were now pulled across the window making it hard to see inside but it seemed clear there were no living creatures stirring in this room. She moved quickly past the door to the next window. Again, curtains were pulled across the window but in the small gaps she could see no movement. Hurrying on to where the hedge met the house, Jane squeezed herself through the tiny gap between the two.

Though the front windows were even more heavily curtained than the back ones had been, this time there was movement. A black and white cat leapt up onto the inside sill. For a moment, their eyes were locked in an eerie staring contest before Jane broke it off. Studying its front paws, Jane saw it wasn't Mittens. After making sure no one on the quiet lane was watching, she ran to the next window. Her appearance at the window once again brought a cat up to the sill. Also, not Mittens. This one was marmalade and white and very superior. It yawned as it watched her trying to see past it into the room beyond. There was nothing else that seemed important, so Jane walked on.

Frustratingly, there was no way up to the second-floor windows, but she felt she'd solved the puzzle. This was a house with facilities for dogs *and cats*. It would have no trouble with two extras.

17

RAMSAY HAS A NEW SUSPECT

"There was a phone call for you, Mr. Ramsay," the B&B owner said, as they entered the house.

Bracken and Ramsay had spent the early hours wandering the fields around the residential home, Ramsay pondering possible alternatives to the missing Mittens story and Bracken ineffectually chasing rabbits. Both were unhappy with the direction their morning had taken by the time they returned.

Ramsay thanked her for the note she handed him and smiled at Morrison's words. He hadn't mentioned police or titles anywhere. The woman offered him the use of her phone but he didn't want anyone listening so he replied, "It may be a long conversation. It's best I don't hog your phone line." He tugged Bracken's leash, and they walked down the road to the public phone box.

Morrison was still at his desk and Ramsay was put straight through. Morrison read out a long list of names that Ramsay noted in his diary. "Thanks for this," Ramsay said. "Austin Westminsters are more popular here in the big city, it seems."

"Do any of the owners' names ring any bells?" Morrison asked.

"Two," Ramsay said, "Aymes and Brereton. Brereton is where I'll start. He's friends with the Tosh I mentioned."

"That Tosh sounds a nasty piece of work, right enough," Morrison said. "Though you should note he has no actual convictions. He must be awfully unlucky in his friends and the places he hangs out."

"Isn't he just," Ramsay said. "I think he has more luck in his legal advisors, though."

"And the pet snatching you asked about," Morrison said. "There aren't many and none sound like the sort of thing you described. More like missing pets or pets the neighbors just grew tired of."

"I thought that would be the case," Ramsay said. "Of these two incidents, the ones I know of, only one has gone to the police, who logged it as a missing pet until the ransom note arrived, and I doubt the other will ever be logged with the police. Though a murder may be caused by it in the days to come."

Morrison laughed. "Be sure it isn't your murder then."

"You'll remember our talk today and inform the local force if it is, won't you?" Ramsay said, chuckling.

Morrison agreed he would, before adding, "I must go. The chief wants me right away."

Ramsay returned to the B&B reviewing the notes he'd made as he went. Bracken walked dejectedly by his side, even more disappointed at this second tame end to the walk. For the first time in all this, Ramsay realized the difficulty he would face asking questions without authority. In his role as police, he could have gone to Mr. Brereton's home and interrogated him without any likely complaint. As Adie's representative, he could ask questions at the residential home too. But as someone without standing, Ramsay could quite likely find the door slammed in his face. Miss Riddell, of course, faced many issues when sleuthing but she had one great advantage. People spoke readily to women, even ones unknown to themselves, when they would wisely refuse to speak to a strange man. Ramsay shrugged. He was acting on behalf of the cat's owner and a car like Mr. Brereton's was seen in the neighborhood. That would have to do as a reason.

As he drove to Brereton's house, he also pondered explaining to Brereton how he knew where Brereton lived. He couldn't say he'd been told by the police or by one of Brereton's acquaintances, so how? The answer came when he arrived at the house. The car was outside and only a mile back down the road, Ramsay had passed a business that sold, groomed, and looked after cats when their owners were away. In fact, the sight of the business so near to Brereton's house was, he felt, more than suspicious enough to warrant attention.

Ramsay rang the doorbell and waited. It was a pleasant, detached house in a good part of town. Whatever Brereton did for a living paid well. He rang the bell again and this time a tall slim man with dark, wavy hair opened the door.

"Yes?" the man asked, puzzled.

He fitted the description he'd been given for Brereton, Ramsay noted, before saying, "I was wondering about this car." He pointed to the Westminster parked beside the door. "Is it yours?"

"What if it is?"

"I've been asked to find a missing cat," Ramsay said, "and a car like this was seen near where the cat went missing."

The man's expression was one of incredulity, but Ramsay had already sensed his body language change.

"I don't know what you're talking about," the man said, beginning to shut the door.

Ramsay put his foot onto the sill to prevent the door closing and continued, "I'm not saying it was your car or that you took the cat but if it was your car, you may have seen something or someone that evening with the cat."

"Look," the man said, "I've told you I don't know anything about this, now get lost." He pushed the door firmly against Ramsay's foot.

Bracken, who'd been fidgeting since they arrived at the door, couldn't stand the tension any longer, began growling quietly.

"It's just," Ramsay said, ignoring the growling at his knee, "along the road is a cattery and here is a car of the kind seen by witnesses on the night a cat went missing. It's a coincidence, of course, but you see how it looks."

"Looks to who?"

"Well, to me," Ramsay said, "and when I tell them, I'm sure the police will agree. I used to be a police officer before I became a private investigator, so I know."

The man paused. "There are lots of cars like mine," he said. "It could have been any one of them."

Ramsay pulled his notebook out of his pocket and said, "An Austin Westminster, dark color with a number like '9 something ANB'. That describes this car very closely, don't you think?"

"Yes, but it describes many others too."

"You see I came to the cattery along the road to ask about the missing cat, and I saw your car. I thought, how coincidental is that. It's too coincidental and here I am asking questions, which if you answer honestly, will satisfy my suspicions. If not, the police will."

"I don't know where this cat went missing from," The man said, "so I don't know if I was parked nearby. How could I?"

"It was a residential home in Clifton," Ramsay said. "Do you know it?"

The man shook his head. He looked amused. "I don't hang around residential homes."

"No elderly relatives needing your visits?"

"None," he said. "Even if I did, I wouldn't visit. Places like that give me the creeps. Satisfied?"

"Not really?" Ramsay said. "What about a missing dog? Do you know anything about that?"

"I don't know anything about it," The man said, though his face had become noticeably paler. "What is this? A woman was asking about a dog only yesterday."

"Then you'll know how dangerous it is for the thief to hold that dog. Now, will anyone remember seeing your car outside that location?"

"No! Now get lost. I've told you everything I know."

As Ramsay had moved his foot, the man was able to slam the door and Ramsay heard bolts being shot into place. He returned to his car, saying, "Well, Bracken, I think you judged that one right. He's another bad 'un and no mistake."

Bracken jumped into the car when the door was open. His whole demeanor that of a dog who'd done his duty and done it well.

They drove back to the cattery where a rather dotty middle-aged woman let Ramsay look over the cats in her care. He saw cats with one white paw, two white back paws, and two white paws on the right or left side, but none that had white fur on both front paws. No Mittens.

He thanked her and drove back to the B&B in time for afternoon tea. He'd phone Miss Riddell when she was home from work.

* * *

THE PHONE RANG and Jane answered. "It's me," Ramsay said. "Is Miss Riddell home?" He heard Jane call her sister and the handset being exchanged.

"Hello, Inspector," Pauline said. "Have you something new?"

"I visited Mr. Brereton today and, while he swears it wasn't, I'm convinced it *was* him who took Mittens," Ramsay replied. "I think that means he probably took Mimi as well."

"But how do we prove it?" Pauline mused.

"Your sister knows him," Ramsay said. "We must use that. Have her call him. Tell him she's going to sell him out to Tosh. If he has sense, he'll produce the dog and get it back to your friend Wendy in a heartbeat."

"That could get Brereton badly beaten, killed even, Inspector," Pauline said, "or, from my point of view, worse, get them on Jane's trail even more than I'm sure they are."

"If you believe that," Ramsay said, "and I fear you're likely right, the sooner you tell this Wendy woman and get the game moving, the safer Jane will be. They'll find her eventually and this way, in their eyes she'll have cleared herself of any involvement."

"It may not," Pauline said. She briefly outlined Jane's friendship with Brereton. "They'll think it no more than a falling out among thieves."

"Still, if she gets Brereton to hand over the dog, they'll go easy on her," Ramsay said. "People like that are violent but it's usually proportionated in their twisted minds."

"You think when he goes to recover Mimi, you'll follow and find Mittens?" Pauline asked, returning to the subject.

"That's exactly what I think and probably other pets, too."

"We should all be ready to follow," Pauline said. "We can't afford any slip ups."

"Your sister will know where he lives and can direct you," Ramsay said. "I'll be there in thirty minutes. It will be a little less for you. Then we find a phone box, Jane talks to him while we watch the house. When he comes out, we follow. Agreed?"

Pauline agreed, hung up the phone and told Jane to dress quickly because they were about to trap her friend Brereton.

"Ramsay really thinks it's Brian?" Jane asked, as Pauline drove swiftly along the quiet evening streets.

"He's sure, and frankly I am too," Pauline said.

"It does look bad, I agree," Jane said, doubtfully, "but I don't see Brian doing this. He must know what Tosh would do to him if he's caught and it isn't like he needs the money. He's loaded."

"Maybe his money is gone," Pauline said. "Maybe it's revenge for some wrong done to him; maybe he just likes the excitement of living dangerously, the way you do."

"Me?" Jane cried. "Who says I like living dangerously?"

"You do," Pauline replied. "Your friends are gangsters and drug dealers and your boyfriends since you arrived here have all been violent."

"Everyone who's anyone must throw themselves about a bit, Pauline. It's how life is at the top. And Zac and Josh were just rough, they weren't really violent."

"You were in hospital, or don't you remember?" Pauline said, exasperated.

"Oh, that. I just landed badly," Jane said, shrugging. "For someone who catches criminals, you're awfully soft, Pauline."

Pauline was saved from replying by seeing the street sign. She pulled over and parked in the darker area between widely spaced streetlights. They had only a few minutes of uncomfortable silence until Ramsay's car pulled up behind Pauline's. She wound down the car window as Ramsay came to talk.

"I'll walk down to his house and confirm he's there. He may already have made himself scarce with my visit on top of your phone call," Ramsay said. "Maybe you can find a phone box. There's sure to be one nearby. I'll be back in five minutes."

Pauline, Jane, and Ramsay arrived back at the cars together. Ramsay confirmed the car was in the drive and the lights were on in the house.

"When he comes out of the street," Pauline said, "we need to have one car ready to go whichever way he turns. I'll drive farther on, turn and park near the phone box. That way Jane can jump in the car and hide before he gets on the road."

"Whichever way he goes, the first car follows immediately," Ramsay said. "The second should wait one minute before following. It would look odd for two cars to suddenly appear behind him on these quiet roads."

Pauline drove slowly forward past the junction with the street and Ramsay saw her brake lights come on a hundred yards farther down the street. He saw Jane get out and disappear behind a hedge where presumably the phone box was located. He returned to his car, started the motor, and prepared to set off in pursuit.

Fifteen minutes later, as he was thinking he should

switch off the engine, he saw Brereton's car arrive at the junction, stop, pull out into the road and drive off past Pauline's car, which immediately began following. He waited until the two cars were out of sight before putting his own car into gear and moving off.

At the first junction, he found they were no longer in sight. Then he saw Pauline's car momentarily between the bushes that obscured his view. He turned to follow and quickly caught up. He mustn't lose them again. Brereton joined the main road to the south and Pauline and Ramsay followed. Ramsay took the opportunity to overtake Pauline and signal to her to fall back. She seemed to understand why he'd done that, and they continued at a good pace. Brereton wasn't speeding but he was driving as fast as the speed limit allowed. Forty-five minutes passed and Ramsay saw him signal to turn off the road into a service station, its Shell sign glowing in the now darkened sky. Ramsay pulled over and parked, waving his arm from the window to catch Pauline's attention. She pulled up behind him.

Pauline jumped out of her car and practically ran to his. "I need to fill up as well," she told him. "I wasn't prepared for him to go this far."

"Me too," Ramsay said. "It seems incredible to me they would be keeping the animals this far away. I think he's running. He doesn't want to be in town when Jane tells Wendy about him and his car's link to the missing pets."

"Does that mean he *knows* what's going on and is afraid, or he *doesn't* know what's going on, and is afraid he won't be able to persuade Tosh he's innocent?"

"Your guess is as good as mine," Ramsay said. "I think, however, it means this plan has not had the desired effect. It hasn't persuaded Brereton to release Mimi, even if he does know where she is."

Pauline nodded. "The more I think about it, the more I think this means he isn't involved. I can't see how this would be his preferred option if he knows where Mimi is."

"I'll follow him when he leaves," Ramsay said. "You fill up. Follow behind as quickly as you can so if I have to pull over, you can continue the chase."

Pauline glanced in the direction Ramsay was looking and saw the attendant handing Brereton his change and stepping back from the car.

Ramsay pulled away after Brereton was far enough down the road to not notice. In his mirror, he saw Pauline turning into the service station.

Ramsay drove on for another thirty minutes before he saw the lights of the car behind flash. He waved his hand, hoping Pauline could see that and began to slow, letting her overtake.

18

A LONG WAY BACK

THE DRIVE SEEMED interminable as the evening grew darker until the last glow of summer light was gone. Wherever he was going, Brereton wasn't stopping to rest before he got there. They were way beyond where keeping kidnapped pets made sense. Pauline realized they had it completely wrong. Whatever Brereton was doing outside the residential home that night, if indeed he was there at all, it wasn't kidnapping cats. Or, if it was, it was on behalf of someone so terrifying that even a gangster like Tosh didn't frighten him.

"I told you it wasn't Brian," Jane said, when Pauline shared her doubts about this chase.

"We need to be sure," Pauline replied, and they lapsed once again into silence.

After midnight, Brereton pulled into another service station and Pauline parked just outside and watched. She was joined a few moments later by Ramsay's car pulling in behind. He'd stopped for fuel some time before and rejoined the chase only minutes earlier. He walked over to her car.

"We were wrong about this, Inspector," Pauline said.

"He's fleeing the city, possibly the country, which tells me he doesn't know anything about Mimi."

"And if he doesn't," Ramsay agreed, "he probably doesn't know about Mittens. We relied too much on the similarity of cars and numbers. I should have known better. Registrations are given in batches. Two or even three numbers, only a digit or so apart, may well be given to a dealer with cars to sell and an Austin dealer may well sell two of the same models and attach license plate numbers only digits apart."

"Do we continue or turn back?" Pauline asked. "I think turn back."

"You should, you have work in the morning," Ramsay said. "I'll go on with him a while longer until I'm certain he's not stopping before London."

Pauline nodded. "You'll phone me tomorrow and let me know, won't you?"

"I will. Now, he's moving again. Good night to you both."

Ramsay quickly ran to his car and drove off, following the Westminster on the road south. Bracken by now was fast asleep, bored with an adventure that left him nothing to do.

BRERETON'S CAR finally pulled off the road around one in the morning and entered a small village where everyone was asleep. Only streetlights showed Ramsay where the car was headed and where it stopped, in a quiet parking spot beside the church.

Ramsay, who'd turned off his lights when entering the village, now pulled into a short driveway where he could watch Brereton. It soon became obvious Brereton had simply pulled off to rest for there was no movement after the Westminster's lights went out. Ramsay walked Bracken, who was anxious to be out of the car, and then they sat and watched as the hours crawled by. Ramsay grumbled occasionally that he'd thought these kinds of nights were over when he'd retired, but Bracken was asleep and made no answer.

When the sky lightened, Brereton made a move, but it was only to drive back out to the major road and continue south with Ramsay following. They were well past Birmingham before Ramsay decided to give up the chase. Brereton was headed to London and the anonymity that came from being one in eight million people. It was still early morning when Ramsay pulled into a service station, filled up the tank, and began the long drive back to Lancashire and the B&B.

19

JANE LEADS THE WAY

As Pauline prepared for work, after barely three hours of sleep, Jane announced she was going to visit the other businesses she'd researched, particularly grooming salons. "I hope you're pleased I'm following your advice not to become focused on just the kennels."

"I am and now follow my other advice and don't do anything foolish," Pauline said, concerned at the expression on Jane's face.

"I don't plan to," Jane said sweetly. "Just see if I can catch them with either of our missing pets."

"I know what happened last night was disappointing," Pauline said earnestly. "We got it wrong. That often happens during an investigation but don't let it encourage you into doing anything illegal."

Jane assured her she wouldn't, and Pauline left for work not wholly reassured.

Once she was sure Pauline was out of the way, Jane left the apartment heading for one of the many pet shops on her list. Nothing foolish, as Pauline had warned, just simply observing. Her morning though was hopelessly disappointing. In a small café, well away from her usual haunts, she nibbled a Chorley cake with a mug of tea, gloomily wondering where to investigate next. A seedy-looking pet shop nearby had been her target, and she could see it from where she sat. In the window a caged rabbit watched an equally cramped, caged poodle that looked nothing like the elegantly coiffed Mimi.

"What an idiot you are, Jane," she said quietly. "Mimi won't look like Mimi here. There won't be bows, pink collar and toenails, no pink blush in her coat. She'll be a scruffy, white poodle. No different to the rest."

She finished her lunch and left the café, crossed the road and studied the poodle in the window. It didn't look like Mimi, but it was almost a week and whoever had her had a strong motive for letting Mimi revert to an unkempt appearance. Inside there may be other poodles.

Jane entered the dimly lit shop. It smelled strongly of animals and her nose twitched in revolt. A disinterested young woman sat behind a counter reading a magazine. Jane nodded to her and made her way to where she could see more dogs in a small pen outside behind the shop. One was a white poodle. Its coat suggested a recent poodle cut and it moved like Mimi. Their mistake over the car was still fresh in her mind, but this dog needed investigating.

Nodding to the server, Jane walked back outside, relieved to be in fresh air again. Quickly, she made her way to the end of the terrace of houses, turned down the side street and into the narrow lane that ran behind the houses until she reached the backyard of the pet shop. She couldn't see in because the owners had built a tall wooden fence to deter trespassers.

The fence was made of vertical planks, which gave her nothing to climb on. She frowned. It had been too many years since she'd clambered up anything, let alone wooden fences in broad daylight. A gap between two planks gave her a finger hold and she tugged at the boards. It moved. Taking a good grip with both hands, she pulled it right off. The gap it left was narrow but by removing her jacket and sweater she was able to wriggle through.

Once in the yard, she found the dogs had noticed her and were gathering to investigate.

"Mimi," she whispered to the poodle that was gazing at her from the back of the crowd, "Mimi."

The dog nearest her barked and immediately the others followed suit. "Mimi," Jane said, "come." The poodle looked uninterested, and the pet shop door opened.

Jane ran to the gap in the fence and began wriggling through. Her blouse buttons caught and held. She stepped back and tried again, holding them flat. One caught again and she had to push it under the plank with shaking hands. She was through and grabbing her clothes when she heard a man shout, "Who's there?"

Jane ran for the corner. As she turned it, she saw a man's head pushing through the gap in the fence. His head disappeared and she realized he was likely going to the shop's front door and would see her if she now stepped out onto the road. She stopped dead, looking along the side street for somewhere to hide. On rough ground farther along the way a thicket of rhododendron bushes was pushing out into the lane. She ran there. With shaking hands, she put on her sweater and jacket. Now she had to wait until the coast was clear. It was a long time before her nerves settled enough for her to feel safe returning to the road and the train station.

Back at the apartment, she poured a large vodka and

flopped onto the couch, where she was sleeping when Pauline came home.

* * *

RAMSAY SLEPT until evening and then walked Bracken again, returning by way of the telephone box where he called Pauline's number.

"Inspector," Pauline said, "what did you learn?"

"That we need something like those German autobahns in this country. Birmingham is a long way by car and London would have been even longer. I turned around somewhere between the two and came home. He's running for the hills, Miss Riddell, not recovering kidnapped pets."

"At least now we know that if he had any part in this, it isn't the principal one."

"And now we're back to the beginning without any new leads," Ramsay said.

"Wait a minute, Inspector," Pauline said, "Jane has an idea who it might be."

Ramsay heard the handset being turned over and then Jane said, "Two, actually."

"Two suspects?"

"Yes," Jane said. "I did some snooping today and while I was getting nowhere, I thought of two crooks I should have thought of earlier."

"Well, you've thought of them now," Ramsay said, patiently. "Who are they?"

"One is a smarmy young creep called Kyle Swalwell," Jane said. "He's muscling in on the kennel business around here. Bringing it into the twentieth century, he says. I don't know why I forgot him; except I never regard him in any way." She paused for breath.

"And the other?"

"This one is more serious," Jane said grimly. "He's too big a crook for this kind of petty crime but maybe he thinks it's worth pursuing because," she paused for dramatic effect, "he's Tosh's newest rival so he might see stealing Mimi as a psychological blow in their growing war."

"What's this one's name?" Ramsay asked. "The local police may tell me more when my old sergeant gives me a friendly name to contact down here."

"His name is Sean Corrigan," Jane said. "He used to be a docker in Salford docks and became the leader of all the thieving from the ships that went on there. Now he controls most of the crime over the Salford side of the river and Tosh has been pushed out and back to the Manchester side."

"Nice," Ramsay said, knowing exactly what 'pushed out' meant in street terms among rival criminal gangs.

"Not nice," Jane said, with a shiver Ramsay thought he could feel through the phone.

"Was Swalwell the kennel owner where you were snooping today?" Ramsay asked.

"Sadly, not," Jane said. "I wasted a day on pet shops and salons. I was so fixated on the lousy kennel I'd heard about from my clients that I missed the obvious. Swalwell's kennels are newer, cleaner, better than the shabby old place I visited, which is good for the dogs, but he's a crook whereas the people I saw yesterday haven't the gumption to try something like petnapping."

"Where might I find this Sean Corrigan?"

Jane told him the little she knew, which was all second-hand from Wendy via Tosh. "But I wouldn't expect him to be the one behind this, Inspector. Like I said, he's big-time now; this will be beneath him."

"Though you also said, Jane. He might see it as an

amusing display of power to steal his rival's wife's dog." Ramsay heard Miss Riddell say something to Jane.

"Pauline asks but why would he take Mittens?"

Ramsay though for a moment. "Maybe he's moving into the entertainment business and sees this as a lever. I don't really know why, yet."

"If you're snooping around Corrigan tomorrow," Jane said, "I'll see if there's anything to be learned at Swalwell's *Kennels for the Caring Owner's Pet*."

"Be careful," Ramsay said. "Don't do anything stupid. No trespassing or anything that might bring you to the attention of this man. You may be wrong and he's just a tough businessman, but you shouldn't test that theory."

After he'd finished speaking to the Riddell's, Ramsay phoned his ex-colleague, Morrison, who'd gone home for the day. He called there and caught him eating his evening meal.

"Look, sir," Morrison said. "I've just sat down to eat. Mrs. Morrison will murder *me* if I spoil this first meal at home for days. I'll phone you back in an hour."

Morrison was punctual. Ramsay's landlady took herself off to another room so they could talk privately.

"Chief Inspector Logan," Morrison said, "you remember him?"

"Jimmy Logan," Ramsay said. "Certainly, I do. I thought he left us for Edinburgh?"

"Too cold, he tells me, so he's back among the Sassenachs but this time in Manchester. Here's the number he gave me." Morrison read it out and Ramsay read it back to him to be sure.

"That's great, man," Ramsay said. "A friend and not just a favor."

Morrison laughed. "Well, you're both Scots so maybe

that makes you friends. He was always a cantankerous old cuss, as I remember, and he wasn't even old."

"We Scots were put on this world to keep you English in order," Ramsay said, chuckling, "and Jimmy took that job seriously." After a further exchange of gossip about the station, Ramsay ended the call.

"Bracken," he said to the collie lying beside the hearth, "tonight you get another walk." His landlady couldn't be expected to stay out of her own sitting room forever and he had no intention of discussing criminals with her listening in. A walk to the phone box at the end of the street would be Bracken's treat.

Jimmy Logan sounded the way Ramsay remembered him. His time in Edinburgh had refreshed his accent that too many years in England had softened.

"You've retired, Ramsay, I hear," Logan said, by way of opening remarks.

"Aye, I have that," Ramsay said, lapsing into his own lost Scots accent, "but I find I'm mixed up in a wee crime. Nothing serious, you understand, just pet snatching for ransom."

"Morrison said. He asked if we'd had anything like that in Manchester. I told him I hadn't heard of any."

"A name that came up in my enquiries," Ramsay said, "is Sean Corrigan. Does that mean anything to you?"

Logan laughed. "Don't play the innocent with me, Ramsay. If that name came up it was with enough background to say this isn't a wee crime"

"Aye, you're right there," Ramsay said, "but I don't yet know what is true and what isn't down here, so I go cautiously with names, do you see?"

"And you should go cautiously with that one, Ramsay. He's not a nice man. Still, this doesn't sound like him. What can you get for a pet ransom? Pennies, at most. Nay, our Sean is well beyond that now."

"The pets involved are more than just Mrs. Smith's Fluffy or Fido," Ramsay said. "These are serious sums of money being asked."

There was a pause before Logan replied, "Then maybe," he said. "If there's the chance to hurt someone as well, it would pique his interest."

"I'm running out of change for the phone box," Ramsay said. "Call me back, please." He gave Logan the number and hung up.

When the call came through, Ramsay quickly asked for information on the other dark-colored, maybe blue, Austin Westminster owners, the creepy kennel keeper Jane had identified, and whatever Logan could give him on Corrigan.

"So, a shopping list of information gathering," Logan said. "How many men do you think I have here?"

"I just want the information that already exists," Ramsay said. "A police clerk should be able to find most of it. Oh, and any gossip on an impresario called Lance Delaval."

"Never heard of him," Logan said. "It sounds like a made-up name."

"It's show business," Ramsay said. "They all have stage names, don't they?"

Logan laughed. "Only to protect the guilty. Seriously, though, Ramsay, you should stay away from Corrigan. People disappear around him."

"What about a man called McIntosh, Tosh for short? I hear he's not a nice man either."

"Are you interested in him too?" Logan asked. "He's as bad as Corrigan. They're two peas in a pod."

"Do people disappear around him as well?"

"Aye, they do. And lose limbs," Logan said. "I find it

impossible to believe either of these two is mixed up in pet snatching. It's not their style. You're on the wrong track, Ramsay. Look at the evidence again and you'll see I'm right."

"I'll do that, Jimmy," Ramsay said. "Meanwhile, whatever you can share will be appreciated."

"I'll see what I can do but don't say I didn't warn you," Logan said. "Just realize I'm not stopping police work for this and whatever you find during your hunt for Mittens, or whatever its name is, I get for our future reference."

"If you're lucky," Ramsay said, "you might get an actual conviction to add to your long and illustrious record."

Logan laughed. "If you go after Corrigan, I'm more likely to get another missing person's report to chase."

On that cheery note, they said goodbye and Ramsay took the impatient Bracken on a long walk around Clifton's few lighted streets.

20

JANE'S LATEST SUSPECT

Jane hopped off the bus and looked around. She knew the address of Creepy Kyle's establishment, but, despite many invitations, she'd never been. Seeing the street name she was searching for, Jane walked until she saw the kennels' sign. As she approached the driveway to the kennels, she could see it was certainly a lot more pleasant than the previous one she'd visited.

Peeping cautiously around the hedge of the neighboring house, she could see no one so Jane strolled past the façade, studying the bungalow as she went. The building was too small to hold many animals, which meant the dogs were being kept in the back. Walking on, she found a lane running between two houses and took that. It soon brought her to the inevitable service lane running behind the houses and she backtracked until she found herself at the kennels. The difficulty was, like at the pet shop, the owner had erected a tall fence and hedge, preventing passers-by looking in and the dogs seeing out. They could hear and smell her though and they began to snuffle and growl. Jane hoped no one was in the yard or she'd be detected, instead of detecting.

At the farthest end of the property was a tall gate set in the hedge. Jane tested the handle; it was locked. She peered through a gap in the hedge, frustrated to be no further forward than she had been with the other kennel. Returning to the front of the bungalow, Jane marched up to the door and rang the bell. A smartly dressed woman answered the door and asked, "Yes?"

"I'm going away for a holiday," Jane lied. "I'm looking at kennels for my dog. She's very special and I want her to think she's on vacation, too."

"Then you've come to the right place, madam," the woman said, stepping aside and inviting her in.

Jane was shown the food preparation area, which she was assured was cleaner than most restaurants and it certainly looked that way and was then led out into the area at the back of the house to the kennel buildings and pens.

"As you see," the woman said, "on fine days we like to let the dogs have their freedom."

"Aren't you worried they may fight?"

"We take good care to learn their ways before they're let out, I assure you madam. There's no chance of your dog coming to any harm."

"If I didn't want my dog outside with the others," Jane said. "What then?"

"We have pens for individual dogs, both outside and inside." They entered through a secure gate into an inner area.

"We always have dogs that can't get along with others, or owners that don't want their dogs mixing," the woman said. "Particularly the females when they're in heat." She smiled and Jane's confidence sank. This was another wasted trip. The kennels were all they were advertised to be.

"Can I see inside the kennel buildings?" Jane asked, as the woman had stopped and didn't look as if she was going further.

"Very well," she said, "but I must ask you not to spread the news if you recognize any of the dogs. Many of the owners who entrust their dogs to us are famous people and wouldn't want it known their dog was here."

"Why?" Jane asked puzzled. "Wouldn't that be good advertising for you?"

The woman sighed. "It would but there's always the risk of someone snatching the dog of a wealthy owner and demanding ransom. We must be very careful."

"I don't know any famous people," Jane said, laughing, "so your secrets are safe with me."

Inside, the building was much lighter than Jane had expected. The roof was translucent, maybe glass, and the sunlight made the central area with separate pens almost as bright as outdoors. Four well-groomed dogs came to greet her, one of which she did recognize. It belonged to a rock musician who was on tour with his band.

"They're beautifully groomed," Jane said, hoping the woman wouldn't notice the obvious signs of recognition the elegant setter was showing toward her. She stroked its head, and it licked her hand. "This one is very friendly."

"He is, isn't he?" the woman said.

Jane thought she detected a note of suspicion in the woman's voice and walked on, looking into every shelter as she went.

"This will do nicely for my darling," Jane said, walking back to the door where they'd entered. "Give me your card and I'll be in touch very soon." As they walked back to the house, Jane took a final look at the building where she'd just been and was immediately struck by how much bigger it was outside than in. She stopped.

"Is there more private area than we visited?" Jane asked the woman.

"Yes, there are two private areas in each building, but they're exactly the same," the woman said. "There's nothing more to see in the other one."

Except different dogs, Jane thought. Should she demand to see inside, or would that just invite suspicion? Deciding it would do exactly that, Jane nodded and continued walking back to the bungalow. She was given a business card, and with more assurances of future business, she left. Heading back to the bus stop, Jane grew more certain that Mimi was in the unseen part of the kennels. The problem now was how to get in there and rescue Mimi. What she needed was a plan.

LATER, when Pauline returned from work, and after Jane had told Pauline of everything she'd seen, Jane asked nonchalantly, as though burglary was an everyday occurrence in the world, "I don't suppose you'd help me go in and find Mimi, Pauline?"

"If by 'go in' you mean 'break in' then you're right," Pauline said. "I won't help you. But we don't need to do that, I could go along at the weekend and get the tour you had. I, however, will have noticed the large size of the building on my way in and ask to see it all."

"You don't know Mimi," Jane objected.

"Which is even better," Pauline replied. "I'll recognize Mimi from the photos you have, but Mimi will not recognize me and give the game away like that setter almost did with you."

"That's true," Jane said, "I hadn't thought of that." She paused before adding, "But I wasn't planning to snatch her, just identify her and get the police to raid the place."

"I'm pleased to hear you saying such sensible things," Pauline added drily. "And the plan will work as well if *I* see Mimi as it would if *you* saw her. Still, even with our identification, we still may need Inspector Ramsay's help for I'm not sure the police will invade private property on the word of two people who have little more than a passing acquaintance with the dog. One poodle looks much like another to most people."

"Mimi and I are friends," Jane cried. "We've known each other for a year now."

"I can see why you think that; it's longer than most of your boyfriends lasted," Pauline said. Seeing the hurt on Jane's face, Pauline wished she hadn't been so unkind. "Sorry," she said. "Bad joke. Put it down to a rotten day at work."

"You can make it up to me by going to the Caring Kennels and taking the full tour," Jane said.

"Not tonight," Pauline replied, "and not so soon after your visit. Thanks to your disguise, we now look alike and two such visits in a short space of time will arouse suspicion if they have Mimi."

"I could dress you as me," Jane said, with a peal of laughter.

"You're supposed to be in hiding," Pauline reminded her. "My being you would tend to give the game away."

Jane continued chuckling. The thought of Pauline in one of her exciting new mini-skirts and makeup was too delicious a thought to let go of.

21

RAMSAY TOO HAS ANOTHER SUSPECT

Ramsay and Bracken reconnoitered the area around Corrigan's principal business address, a dilapidated warehouse at Salford Docks. Even on this sunny day, coal soot lay on everything giving a greyish abandoned cast to the place. That it was still in use was obvious, loading doors were open and a vehicle was backed inside being stacked with goods.

Ramsay knew from long experience around Newcastle's docks that the men working around the loading bay were regular workers and likely to be Corrigan's irregular brawlers. The real villains, however, the ones the police could never catch, were in offices and backrooms well out of sight. Unfortunately, a man without coveralls and walking a dog was too conspicuous for getting a closer inspection. He needed to come back alone and in suitable workmanlike attire.

A red jaguar, pulled up at the side of the building. Ramsay continued walking, his eyes fixed firmly on its occupants as they stepped out and made their way into the building. The older, burlier man in the sharp suit had to be

Corrigan, or at least one of his highest accomplices. He noted the car number, color, and make in his notepad before continuing his circumnavigation of the warehouse. By the time he'd completely circled the building, he'd further noted additional entrances and office windows. None looked secure but, he thought wryly, no one would burgle the known headquarters of a local gang boss.

Returning to his car, he drove away far enough to feel that he wasn't being followed and found a telephone box where he phoned Logan. His old friend confirmed the Jaguar did belong to Corrigan and agreed Ramsay's description of the car's most notable occupant did sound like Corrigan.

"And the shopping list I gave you?" Ramsay said. "Anything to report there?"

"Report! I don't report to you, old friend."

Ramsay hurriedly apologized for his poor use of the word and said, "Still, has anything interesting turned up?"

"Delaval," Logan said, "is struggling, they say, and he's become a drug addict. Could just be gossip. He hasn't been arrested."

"I'll keep that in mind, thanks," Ramsay said. "What about Kyle Swalwell?"

"We've never heard of him," Logan said. "Who is he?"

"He's a kennel owner and a person of interest," Ramsay said. "Anything you have would be helpful."

Logan laughed and reminded Ramsay there were laws against wasting police time, before ending the call.

Now he knew who and what to look for, Ramsay set off for home and the hills where Bracken could stretch his legs. As they walked on the low hills around Clifton, he considered the two suspects Jane had suggested. He could imagine the dodgy kennel owner stealing the pet of a harmless man like Magic Mal, but it was inconceivable he'd steal the pet of a gangster's wife. He could imagine an up-and-coming gangster like Corrigan tweaking the nose of a rival he considered past it but while it was possible, it was truly unlikely. And he couldn't see either of them being behind a pet snatching ring here in the north-west. Were these two separate crimes? That too was unlikely, or it was an amazing coincidence. There was no direct connection between Wendy and Mal, he was sure of that, and Mr. Lance Delaval was a tenuous link at best. But if neither of the two new suspects, creepy Kyle or criminal Corrigan, were the head of this ring, then it was unlikely they were even involved. At most, Kyle's kennel was where the pets were hidden but that was all.

"Well, Bracken, what say you to walking past the residential home one more time?"

Bracken liked any idea that allowed him to sniff out the many scents of the countryside, lamp posts, street corners, and other marking spots for dogs and happily trotted alongside.

At the residential home, Ramsay was pleased to see the janitor leaving for the day.

"Do you remember him, Bracken?" Ramsay whispered softly.

Bracken growled quietly, confirming he did.

"I think we'll follow him to his house and see what we find there," Ramsay continued softly. The Janitor didn't seem to notice his tail as he trudged, head down, into the village where he stopped at the local shop. Minutes later, he left the shop, lighting a cigarette. Ramsay and Bracken had hidden themselves in a small alleyway running off the main street. It was well they did because the janitor crossed the road and would have seen them if they hadn't been out of sight.

Ramsay watched the man set off down a lane between two houses on the other side of the road and followed when he felt confident he wouldn't be seen. About a hundred yards down the lane, the janitor unlocked the door to a modest cottage and disappeared inside. Ramsay and Bracken approached the cottage quietly, and being careful as they passed its window, circled around it to get the lay of the land.

Satisfied he had a good grasp on the cottage's entrances and windows, Ramsay returned to the main road.

"We'll visit after our walk and on our way back to the B&B," he said. "You can sniff out Mittens, if she's on the premises."

Bracken seemed unsure of the value of this offered treat. His expression didn't suggest he relished the plan.

Seeing Bracken's lack of enthusiasm, Ramsay said, "Well, I can't so it must be you. I suppose it would help if we had something of Mittens' to give the scent. We'll return to the residential home. Adie will have a collar or blanket we can use."

Adie had a blanket from Mittens' basket. Thanking her, Ramsay and Bracken set out for the B&B and on the way revisited the janitor's cottage. Ramsay let Bracken sniff the blanket before letting him off the leash to investigate alone. Bracken hunted for a trail up to the cottage door, then around the building before returning to sit at Ramsay's feet.

"I'll take that to mean you didn't find anything," Ramsay said, disappointed. The janitor handing the cat over to the people in the car that was parked near the residential home had always been the most likely explanation, but he'd hoped maybe Mittens was still with the man. Bracken not finding a scent didn't prove she wasn't, but it did suggest it was the car he needed to find.

As they walked back to the B&B, Ramsay said, "I have a glimmer of an idea, Bracken. We need to know about more of the staff."

Bracken, who was beginning to tire, didn't lift his head. He'd had enough sleuthing today and none of it had been interesting.

The B&B owner appeared in the hall the moment he entered the house. It seemed to him she always did. Her radar for guests must be finely tuned, Ramsay thought. Or was it just unattached male guests?

"Good evening," she said brightly. "Your dinner will be another thirty minutes, I'm afraid. I was expecting you at your usual time."

"That's quite all right," Ramsay replied, smiling. "I need to freshen up anyway." He hurried upstairs to his room and waited until he heard the crockery being moved about before descending the stairs.

"Are you still looking into the missing cat?" his landlady asked.

"Yes, why? Do you know something I should know about?"

She shook her head. "Not really, I'm just curious."

A thought struck him, and he asked, "Do you know any of the staff at the residential home?"

"A little," she replied. "They live here in the village, and we know each other to say hello."

"There's a nice nurse who I've met when I visit Adie, the woman who had the cat when it went missing. Nurse Carey, I remember. Do you know her?"

"Oh, yes," his landlady replied. "She's lived here almost all her life. Poor woman. Her newlywed husband was killed in the war. She never really got over it."

As this was Ramsay's own experience, and Miss Riddell's

too, he found it difficult to respond beyond, "I can understand that."

"The one to watch there," his landlady said, "is their janitor. He's a rogue if ever there was one."

"In what way?"

"Oh, the usual kind of things. Things that fall off the back of lorries, for example. He always has toasters to sell, as well as other things he couldn't have come by honestly."

Ramsay laughed. Every community seemed to have one or more of those characters. A petty criminal that everyone tolerated because the level of dishonesty was too low for the full majesty of the law, and they were useful. If you wanted something that you couldn't afford, the local rogue could generally get it at a price you could pay.

"You think pet snatching is something he might do?"

"I would say so," the landlady replied. "Right up his street, that would be. I'd advise you to buy him a drink or a bottle of something and the cat would be back by morning."

Ramsay nodded. As this had been his impression from the moment he'd seen the janitor, he felt a surge of optimism and relief. There was no mastermind at work here, just a sneak thief looking for some petty cash. Only the ransom demanded wasn't petty cash so how could he explain that?

"I shall consider your suggestion carefully," he said. "I'd like a happy ending to this rather spiteful little puzzle." Even with the certainty he felt that this was a petty crime, Ramsay couldn't quite believe the janitor would ask for ten thousand pounds. It was so far out of the range of money such a man experienced; it would seem like madness to him to even ask for it.

"You should," she replied. "A much more likely thief than poor Mrs. Carey."

"You say 'poor Mrs. Carey'," Ramsay said. "Why is that?"

"Well, just the way her life has gone really. Twenty years ago, she was the bride of an army captain and looking forward to a good life with the war coming to an end. Then she was widowed and has had to make her own way on a nurse's pay. Her parents died and they had little to leave among their children. Now she's nursing in an old folk's home with no prospects to look forward to but a lonely old age."

Ramsay, who thought it sounded very much like his own situation, was irritated by this bleak view of what he had no doubt Mrs. Carey would think was a blameless and useful life. As he did of his own.

"I think she sounds a sensible, hard-working woman who might well feel she's had a full life, helping others as she does," he said somewhat sharply.

"I dare say," the landlady replied, "but it can't have been what she was expecting or hoping for and I'm sorry for her."

Realizing he would grow angry if this continued, Ramsay changed the subject. When the meal was over, he returned to his room still on tolerable terms with his landlady.

22

INVESTIGATING CARING KENNELS

PAULINE KNOCKED on the door of the Caring Kennels, and when a man opened it, introduced herself as a dog owner looking for a superior place for her pet to stay while she visited relatives down south. She was relieved the person giving the tour wasn't the woman Jane had described because it meant that nothing Pauline said would jog the woman's memory of Jane's visit.

The tour followed much the same itinerary that Jane described so it was clearly the kennels regular introduction for prospective clients. When they'd seen the one pen of the inside area, the man was about to lead her out when Pauline asked, "Isn't there more to this building?"

The man agreed there was but added, "It's only extra private rooms for our guests."

"Private? For dogs?"

"Some owners don't want people to know their dogs are here," the man said. "It's security for the dogs and the owners, you see."

"And you have some special dogs with you right now?"

"We always have," he said. "We're the kennels for people who are somebody. Our clients appreciate that."

Pauline smiled. "I'd never have thought of it, but I suppose it's true. It would be a giveaway to a dishonest person if they saw a celebrity dog in the kennels."

"Honest people don't think of these things," her tour guide agreed, "because we don't have to. Nobody knows us, our pets, or where we live. It isn't the same for the rich and famous."

Pauline laughed. "It's fortunate for us we aren't rich and famous. I shall try to remember that next Monday morning when I get up for work. Can I peek in the rest of the pens? It's just plain old curiosity but I would like to see the lifestyles of rich and famous dogs."

He looked about to refuse but then shrugged. "Why not. Maybe you'll consider putting your own pet in our special section. Though I must warn you, they are expensive. Still, for a loved one, expense isn't the determining factor, is it?" He smiled, his manner returning to a salesman talking to a valued client.

They entered the restricted area and Pauline knew at once Mimi wasn't there. Not one dog was a poodle. The rich and famous ran to more exotic breeds.

"Beautiful dogs," Pauline said, as they left the area, and he locked the door behind them. "I imagine if I read society magazines, I might recognize the dogs and then guess the owners. It's a sensible precaution to take."

He nodded. "Your own dog would, I'm sure, fit in well with the others and consider this – you may meet an owner when you arrive or leave, and that connection might help you in your own life. It might even be thought the expense was an investment."

Pauline smiled. "You make a persuasive case and I'll

certainly look at the possibility, but I feel everyday kennel life will have to do for my darling."

Outside, Pauline looked at the second building with its own outdoor pen. "The other building is the same?"

He nodded. "Exactly the same. We don't make a distinction except for the dogs of people who need security."

The pen and building did look identical and the dogs she could see outside were also similar. Pauline nodded. "Thank you for the tour. You've convinced me this is the place."

She accepted the business card and price sheet he offered, promised an early call and booking, and bade him goodbye.

Back at the car, an impatient Jane demanded to be told every detail of what she'd seen. Pauline described the visit and the dogs she'd seen in the indoor area.

"I knew it," Jane cried triumphantly. "The other building is where the stolen pets are kept. That's why they only take visitors to the first one."

"We don't know anything of the sort," Pauline reminded her, as she drew away from the curb and into traffic. "But what I do know is Mimi wasn't in the building I saw."

"It's the other building. Now when do we break in and prove it?" Jane asked. "I say tonight. We can't lose any more time."

"I think we should have Inspector Ramsay get his friend involved," Pauline said.

"I'm always hearing from the family about how you break into places and set traps for murderers," Jane said. "Why so craven this time?"

"I'm not as foolish as I was in the beginning," Pauline said hotly. Stung by the scorn in Jane's voice. "I've learned discretion."

"I haven't," Jane replied. "I'm going in tonight and you can help or stay at home pretending you know nothing."

"Breaking into kennels where dozens of dogs are kept will be almost impossible to do quietly," Pauline pointed out. "The dogs will bark the place down and we'll be arrested for breaking and entering."

"Not if we take treats," Jane said, "and wait until dogs and humans are asleep."

"We need a plan to get in quietly," Pauline said, "and a plan to get out with Mimi if she's there."

"And Mittens if she's there," Jane reminded her.

"I don't think they'd mix up dogs and cats like that. There's too much potential for things to go wrong."

"Then Mimi tonight and Mittens when we find where they're keeping the other pets they've snatched."

At one o'clock in the morning, everywhere was quiet around Caring Kennels. Every house on the street was in darkness. Pauline and Jane quietly stepped out of the car and made their way to the gate that allowed access to the grounds. The hinges groaned, as if woken from their sleep, when Pauline swung the gate carefully open. Pushing it closed behind them, they crossed the backyard toward the door into the building that held the pets of the stars.

Its door was locked but Pauline had learned from cases past how to pick a lock with a hairgrip and the door was soon opened. They'd agreed that because Jane knew Mimi, she would go inside while Pauline watched for passersby and guarded the door.

Jane was only gone two minutes before she was back. 'The inner door is locked too," she whispered.

They made their way through the darkened building

using the faint light from the moon that shone through the glass ceiling above and the narrow beam of Pauline's small flashlight, which was all she felt safe using while burgling. All around, dogs snuffled and snored but seemed not to notice their presence.

With the door open, Pauline returned to the outer door while Jane went in search of Mimi. This did begin to awaken some dogs and Pauline heard whining and growling that threatened to rouse the others. She imagined Jane handing out treats like candies while she made her way from pen to pen. If she was, it wasn't working because the sounds were growing louder.

Then she heard Jane call, "Mimi!"

Dogs began to bark, and Pauline heard noises inside the bungalow. She was ready to go in search of her sister when Jane appeared at the door.

"She's not there," she whispered. More dogs were barking now, and Pauline pulled the door shut behind Jane.

"Let's go," she said, "and quickly."

They ran to the gate, as a light came on inside the bungalow. In turning to see if anyone was at a window, Jane tripped and fell. Pauline fell over her. They scrambled to their feet as they heard a door being opened and hadn't reached the outer gate before a man's voice shouted, "Stop!"

They ignored him and fled through the gate, though Pauline remembered to close it behind her, and ran down the lane to the road where their car was parked. They'd parked well away from the kennel property, thinking it best not to have the car identified with the kennels, but now, Pauline realized, it could become a serious problem. Neither of them was a fast runner and the man could easily catch them if he were.

"I can't keep this up," Jane gasped as Pauline came alongside.

Pauline grabbed her arm and tugged her along. "You have to," she said. "That man could be after us."

At the car, Pauline fumbled with the door key, unable to hit the keyhole she was shaking so much. With the driver door open, she leapt inside, leaned across the gear lever and passenger seat to let Jane in. As Jane flopped in the seat, Pauline turned the key. The engine coughed, started running fitfully and stopped.

"No," Pauline cried, turning the key again, more forcefully this time.

Milly's engine started, hiccoughed. Pauline held her breath, and the engine began in earnest. She shifted into gear and drove off as quickly as she dared, without, she hoped, raising the suspicions of anyone looking out to see what the commotion was at the kennels.

Once they were safely away, Jane began to laugh.

"Are you mad?" Pauline cried.

"I've just learned I need to become a lot fitter before I begin my own career as a sleuth," Jane said, still giggling. "You're years older than me and would have left me in the dust if I wasn't your favorite baby sister."

"You're not my favorite anything right now," Pauline said crossly.

"Pooh!" Jane said. "We got into the place and out without any harm to either of us. I don't know why you're upset. It's just a shame Mimi wasn't there. Where do you think they're keeping her?"

"What dogs were in there?"

"Two beautiful wolfhounds," Jane said, "a Samoyed, and a Great Dane. I know the last two, which is why they were getting excited. They probably thought I'd come to take them home."

"Fortunately for us, they can't speak," Pauline replied.

"Did you recognize the man?" Jane asked.

Pauline shook her head. "I only saw his silhouette against the light. The question is, if it was the man who showed me around, did he recognize me?"

"It was too dark," Jane said, "and in pants and windcheater, you wouldn't look anything like your appearance when you visited before."

"I hope you're right," Pauline said. "If they're criminals, they'll have ways of finding us. You can be sure of that."

"I don't see how," Jane retorted.

Pauline almost growled in frustration at Jane's naiveté. "They'll soon make the connection between two women having a tour and then two women breaking into their property."

"How would they know we were the same people," Jane said. "In the dark, anybody can be anybody."

"Not quite anybody, even shadows and silhouettes are identifiable," Pauline said, "and whatever they pretend in books and films, people can tell women from men even in the dark."

Jane laughed. "You're right. If we couldn't, none of us would be here. But seriously, Pauline, it must be them, even if we didn't find Mimi this time. I know you say to keep an open mind, and I'm getting better at that, but none of the other places come close to this one as a possible hiding place for Mimi."

Pauline shook her head. "If Mimi isn't there, it can't be them. Let's think."

23

RAMSAY SPIES ON A GANGSTER

Ramsay was up early and out to the phone box in time to speak to Miss Riddell before she set out for work.

"You're early, Inspector," Pauline said.

"It's the early bird that catches the worm, Miss Riddell," Ramsay began, before Pauline interjected.

"Perhaps you could tell Jane."

Ramsay laughed. "Our novice sleuth is still in bed?"

"She is." Pauline chuckled. "No investigating before noon is Jane's work schedule."

"Don't people need pets groomed in the mornings?"

"Clearly not Jane's clients. They're probably just getting home at this time," Pauline replied.

"Well, while our partner sleuth was resting, I went to Mr. Corrigan's establishment," Ramsay said. "It's a warehouse in the docks. It could be used to hold stolen pets; the noise from the ships and cranes would smother any sounds from the animals but it's not a place for the faint-hearted."

"Hmm," Pauline said. "Jane is brave but she's also impetuous and foolhardy." She told him of their narrow escape at the kennel incursion of the previous evening. "I'd prefer we went without Jane."

"Miss Riddell," Ramsay said, "you both behaved unwisely, not just Jane. You can be sure Corrigan's men won't be as gentle as the kennel owners if they were to catch us in their warehouse. Breaking and entering is a crime in this country or had you forgotten?"

"But something must be attempted," Pauline responded. "We must find enough evidence to have the police raid the place."

"The police have been trying to get evidence for some time now," Ramsay said. "Like all his kind, they know how to keep their criminality far away from themselves. We wouldn't do any better, no matter how many laws we broke."

"If that's true, then the pets aren't likely to be in the warehouse," Pauline replied.

"Nor his home, which I've also been able to locate. It's not so far away from Clifton, by the way," Ramsay said.

"He's moved up in the world," Pauline said. "Dockworker to country estate."

"Another two generations and they'll be knights of the realm," Ramsay agreed, laughing.

"If it's him," Pauline said, "there must be another place you haven't found yet. I'll see what people know where I work. We should talk again tomorrow."

With that agreed, Ramsay hung up the phone and said to the patiently waiting Bracken, "Now, we'll walk."

The ever-patient Bracken trotted alongside Ramsay as they strolled out into the countryside, each occasionally speaking to the other but neither being understood, except in the general way of contented friendship.

"You know, Bracken," Ramsay said, after a long period of contemplation, "even if it is Brereton behind Mittens' disappearance. I'm sure the cat isn't down south with him. It's hereabouts, which means someone local knows Brereton. More than knows him, has a close enough relationship with him for them to risk this enterprise together."

Bracken gave him a quizzical look, shook his head, and uttered a soft bark.

"You'd already figured that out, had you?" Ramsay said. "Pity, then, you didn't tell me."

Bracken ignored him and followed his nose down a promising trail.

"But if Mittens is being kept local, why did they even need Brereton? Why didn't that sneaky caretaker just take Mittens to the house of his accomplice? You see what I mean?" His question was addressed to Bracken who, understanding his presence was required, gave up on the scent and returned to Ramsay's side.

"I'll have to think on it, Bracken," Ramsay said, "and I can do that while we go out to Corrigan's house to spy out the land." He turned, and they made their way quickly back to the B&B and his car.

24

THE KENNELS ARE CLEAN

PAULINE WOULD HAVE BEEN ASTONISHED to find her sarcasm about Jane sleeping late was not true on this occasion. Almost the moment Pauline left the apartment, Jane phoned Ramsay, who was out.

Leaving a message for him with the B&B owner, Jane prepared breakfast while she thought about the clothes she should wear on this new incursion into the very first kennels she'd watched in the rain. Whatever Pauline said, this was the best place for stolen cats and dogs to be hidden and Jane hadn't yet ruled them out of *her* investigation. Jane loved the *The Avengers* on television and had an extensive wardrobe of Cathy Gale hip hugger pants. Unfortunately, they were among the clothes torn to shreds in her vandalized apartment. All she had with her was the leather suit like the one Cathy used in most of the fight scenes, and which Jane wore to parties. It would look odd on the bus and street, however.

Deciding that, odd as it might look to people on the street, she might indeed need to fight her way out and the leather suit was what she would wear. Wearing her tan duffel coat on top would hide most of the ornamental belts, straps and buckles the designer had felt necessary to add.

Ramsay still hadn't phoned by the time Jane was dressed and ready to go. She wrote Pauline a note explaining where she would be if she wasn't home before Pauline returned from work. It gave her a funny feeling writing the note. If she wasn't home, it probably meant she was dead. She had a faint hope of being held captive while the villains cleaned up the evidence of their crime and ran away, but she knew that was nonsense. Once she was caught there could only be one outcome because the villains wouldn't leave a witness alive; upsetting someone like Tosh was suicidal. This sobering thought almost made her call the enterprise off. Only knowing Pauline had taken similar risks in the past helped her fold the note and place it where Pauline would find it when she returned home.

What had once seemed a slow bus ride out to the kennels now whizzed by too fast and she was soon on the road outside the house mulling her next move. She'd imagined two courses of action. The first, ring the doorbell and confront whoever opened the door with photos of Mimi and Mittens. The second was even more risky. If no one was about, force her way into the kennels and house – she was sure she knew enough now which of the buildings to enter – grab the two pets and run for it, hoping the other animals wouldn't make enough noise to alert the neighborhood.

Staring at the front door, however, both courses of action seemed like madness and not to be attempted without armed support. Deciding to put off her decision until after she'd once again seen the kennels and the rear of the building, she made her way down the lane she'd used on her previous visits. No one was at the back either. Jane frowned. The windows too showed no sign of movement or lights inside. Where were these people? They wouldn't leave pets unattended, would they? If the owners learned their pets were locked in all day while the kennel owners were out, the business would be bankrupt when word got around.

Now, with her plan of breaking and entering staring her in the face, she hesitated. Jane checked the lane for passersby and there were none. It was a sleepy late summer afternoon in the suburbs. Deciding Cathy Gale wouldn't waste time dithering, Jane took off her duffel coat and hung it on a branch of the hedge. She checked both ways again. Still no one. With a firm push, she opened the fence gate and stepped into the garden.

No one was moving at the windows of the house. That should have been reassuring but it made her even more nervous. Were they watching and waiting to pounce?

Jane quickly crossed the open area to the gate into the dog pens, the place she was sure housed the kidnapped pets. It was locked but low enough for her to climb over, made easier by the leather pants that wouldn't tear if she caught them on the spikes. *Thanks, Cathy*, was the thought that flashed through her head; it made her giggle.

The kennel door wasn't locked and opened easily as she stepped inside. She pulled the door closed behind her, just leaving it open enough to watch the house, which she did for a minute before walking quickly through the building. In the pens at either side of the walkway, dogs that had been resting on straw matting rose and came to sniff at her through the chain link fence. She talked quietly to them, reassuring them she meant no harm and they responded as she'd hoped by staying silent.

"Mimi," Jane called in a low voice.

Apathetic dogs raised their heads and gazed at her, but none answered to the name Mimi. The lethargic reaction of the dogs made Jane suspicious. Were they doped to keep them quiet? It would make sense if they were stolen pets.

She began examining each dog carefully in turn, walking among the pens looking for poodles. She found one but it wasn't Mimi. Jane made her way slowly back outside, trying not to startle or excite the animals. Now she could see all the dogs were slow and detached from their surroundings. Most un-dog-like.

With still no activity from the house, Jane made her way to the next building. Now she knew how the dogs were being kept quiet, she was a lot more confident moving around and calling for Mimi. The result was the same. Worse, there were only dogs here so if this was a place to keep kidnapped pets, they were only dog thieves.

She left the building and stared at the house. Would they go away and leave a door or window unlocked? She thought not.

"Nothing ventured, nothing gained," she said quietly to herself and moved to the back door of the house. It was locked. So were the windows at either side. She frowned, then grinned. There was always one window left open in every house, the toilet window. No one liked smells going inside, no matter what the weather. On a sunny day like this, the window would be open.

She hurried around to the side where she remembered the toilet to be and was pleased to see her prediction was correct. The larger, lower window was closed and locked, but the smaller, upper window was open enough to slide her fingers inside and lift the locking bar. Standing on the window ledge, Jane could get her head and one shoulder through the small window and unlatch the lower one. She jumped down and opened the window. *If I ever decide to give up pet grooming, I'll be a burglar.*

Inside the house was quiet. No guard dogs came to greet her as she swiftly moved from room to room on the ground floor. There was nothing to be found. Jane made her way quickly upstairs, her heart thumping, expecting to hear a car return or a door being opened. The doors of the upstairs rooms were closed. Opening the first, she discovered why. Two elegant Persian cats jumped down from a bed and headed straight for the door. Jane closed it quickly and heard the cats hissing and scratching on the other side.

She had the same experience at the next room but this time she was prepared and only stuck her head around the partly open door. A large tabby cat eyed her from the windowsill but made no effort to escape. On a dresser, up near the ceiling, Jane saw a black-and-white cat that, for a moment she thought may be Mittens. It wasn't. Its front paws were both black. She closed the door and moved to the next room.

The last room was the same. Cats but no Mittens. Jane examined the ceiling above the corridor she was in. There was a trapdoor, undoubtedly leading into an attic, but it looked painted over, without any sign of it being opened recently. Her fear of detection was now reasserting itself. With the whole house searched, she had to face the truth. Whatever she thought about this kennel's owner, he wasn't keeping stolen pets here and she should leave before he returned.

Her return to the gate and her duffel coat were as uneventful, and disappointing, as her search had been. Slipping on her coat, she returned to the bus stop and her journey home with but one thought running through her head: *So much for Jane the great detective.*

25

SLEUTHS GETTING NOWHERE

From a safe distance, Ramsay watched the Clifton Manor day workers leaving. When he saw the pleasant nurse leave, he tugged Bracken's leash and they set off in pursuit, keeping a deniable distance between him and her. If the janitor had been the means of getting the cat out, maybe the nurse was where the cat was being kept.

He didn't have far to go. She lived in a small bungalow at the farther end of the village. When she was safely inside, Ramsay and Bracken walked past the front gate – dog and owner on their afternoon exercise. If Ramsay had expected to see Mittens sitting in the front windows of the house, he would have been disappointed, for she wasn't. Fortunately, he assumed if the nurse was holding the cat, she'd know enough not to let it be seen at the windows looking out onto the street where any passerby might recognize it. He noted a small footpath leading up the side of the house and disappearing into bushes. Scanning the field as they followed the path, Ramsay finally saw what he wanted to see. A joining path that he could come back along so he would have a reasonable excuse for being at the rear of the bungalow.

His return did indeed bring him where he wanted to be. He could see the nurse working in what was no doubt the kitchen with a bay window looking out onto a nicely kept lawn and garden. There was no Mittens, or any other cat, in either window at this side of the bungalow. Nor were there pet bowls outside on the small patio at the kitchen door. Ramsay let Bracken sniff the corner of the garden wall and he learnt a lot of what went on there in the dog world. Nothing, however, spoke to Bracken of cats. Ramsay knew this because Bracken was funny about cats, part curious, part aggressive, and part defensive. Ramsay suspected he'd had a run in with a farmyard cat early in his life.

"Not the nurse, then, Bracken," Ramsay said, tugging at the leash. "Let's wander on down the street. Who knows, we may just see Mittens sitting in a window, you never know."

They didn't and Ramsay and Bracken returned to the B&B happily tired from their walk, but in Ramsay's case, unhappily frustrated with his lack of progress. Today had felt like he was chasing phantoms.

After his evening meal, Ramsay phoned Pauline's number and got Jane who told him in detail of her successful day eliminating one kennel owner from their enquiries.

When he could speak, Ramsay said sternly, "As I told your sister, it's fortunate for both of us I'm no longer in the police. I would have to report your breaking and entering."

"Nonsense," Jane said. "We have a duty to catch these villains before they do more harm. Investigating is what we do."

"There are rules concerning private property," Ramsay said, "and it sounds like you broke every one of them today."

"Well, you aren't in the police," Jane retorted, "so what's

our next move? If we're going to catch these people before the pets are killed, we must act faster than this."

"We could watch Corrigan's country property," Ramsay began.

Jane interjected, "What property?"

Realizing he'd taken a wrong step – Pauline hadn't shared that with her sister – Ramsay said mildly, "I know where Corrigan lives when he's not watching over his criminal enterprises around the docks."

"Tomorrow then," Jane said. "We search the place when they're out."

"It's a big property," Ramsay said. "Even if Corrigan and his missus go out, there are servants and staff still there. We can't search the premises without being seen by somebody."

"I need a disguise," Jane mused. "A council inspector checking drains maybe?"

Ramsay laughed. "No! That would never work."

"Well, I'll think of something tonight that *will* work, and you can pick me up in the morning."

"We can observe the place tomorrow morning if you wish," Ramsay said, "but there won't be any illegal entering while I'm with you. Is Pauline there?"

"She can't stop me," Jane said. "I'm beginning to doubt you two had any success in solving crimes. You're both so slow you couldn't catch cold."

"I'm not taking you unless you promise to stay within the law," Ramsay said, "and I wanted to talk to Pauline for her thoughts, not to have her restrain you."

He heard a muffled agitated conversation before the handset was passed to Pauline.

"I wish you hadn't told Jane about Corrigan's country house," Pauline told Ramsay angrily the moment she had the phone. "Now she wants to break in and confront him there. She's sure that's where the pets are being kept."

"Your sister is hot-headed," Ramsay agreed, "but as I recall you were equally drawn to getting close to dangerous criminals when you were starting out."

"But I'm a steadier character," Pauline retorted, thinking how lame that sounded.

Ramsay laughed. "Of course you are. I'll go with her and see she doesn't get into serious danger."

With that, Pauline had to be satisfied, though she doubted Ramsay could stop Jane in full pursuit of anything she'd set her heart on. No one else had been able to.

"Jane said you wanted my thoughts, Inspector," Pauline said. "On what?"

"I'm at a dead end with my Mittens search," Ramsay replied. "And you and Jane don't seem to be very much farther than that on Mimi. I wanted to see if we can't find a new lead in all we've learned."

"I've been thinking about the ransom demands," Pauline said. "Why haven't the kidnappers set a time and place to hand over the loot?"

"In Magic Mal's case, it's because he's having trouble raising the money," Ramsay replied. "They're holding off until he says he has it."

"Is that normal?"

"I don't know. This is England; kidnappings are rarer than sunny days. The kidnappers appear lost to me. They don't know what to do. As lost as we are trying to find them."

"Then I say we tell Magic Mal to say he has the money when they next phone and we catch them at the pickup point."

"If he doesn't hand over money, and we don't catch them when he hands over an empty bag, then Mittens is dead, Miss Riddell," Ramsay said. "This is a risky strategy."

"It's been a week now," Pauline replied. "Mittens can't have too many cat lives left at this point, if any."

"You're concerned Jane will do something risky," Ramsay said, "but your plan is equally risky."

"Jane's plan risks losing her life. Mine risks losing a cat's life. The risks may be the same, but the consequences aren't."

"I'm not sure Magic Mal would agree with you," Ramsay said with a laugh. "After all, he doesn't know Jane."

"You don't like my suggestion, so what's yours?" Pauline said rather crossly.

"You're right," he said. "I called for thoughts and I'm not keen on the answer. Not helpful."

"What about Brereton," Pauline asked. "I know we decided he isn't involved but what if we're wrong and he is? Can't we use him to lead us to the pets?"

"He's in London," Ramsay said. "Or at least he's somewhere down that way," he added thoughtfully. "The call to Wendy was made by a man, Jane said."

"Exactly," Pauline began but was interrupted by Jane.

"Wendy would recognize Brian's voice," Jane said. "It can't have been him. Forget Brian. He isn't that stupid."

"So you say but someone is. What about that janitor?" Pauline suggested. "Could Brereton be working with him and told him who to phone and what to say?"

"He would phone from a phone box," Ramsay said, "so there's no hope of tracing the calls to him if he did."

"They might be able to say where the call came from though," Pauline continued. "Who else in the village of Clifton would be involved?"

"We'd need the date and times of the phone calls,"

Ramsay said. "Mal might be able to remember. Would Jane's friend Wendy?"

"Tosh got a note and Wendy got a phone call," Jane reminded him. "I'll ask when we finish this call." She was standing at Pauline's side, determined not to be left out.

"And I'll phone Magic Mal," Ramsay said, preparing to go. "Phone me at the B&B when you have something."

"And you be here in good time tomorrow," Jane said. "I want to see Corrigan's country place."

Ramsay sighed. Like Miss Riddell, he now also wished he hadn't told Jane.

"No disguises, no housebreaking," he said. "Those are my rules."

Jane made suitably reassuring noises and hung up. She phoned Wendy and asked when the ransom note arrived and the date of the later phone call. She didn't hold out a lot of hope for this, Wendy being Wendy, so she was surprised when Wendy provided both dates.

"That's great," Jane said. "Particularly the note. We can eliminate those who weren't in town that day."

"I've thought of this already," Wendy replied. "It doesn't help; someone could have delivered the note for them. And your sister said she'd told Brian to get in touch, but I still haven't heard from him. I went to his house, and he wasn't there. Can you tell me where I'll find him?"

Fortunately, Jane thought, *I can be honest.* "If he isn't at home, I don't know where he is. We did tell him you wanted to speak to him, but we haven't spoken to him since."

"If he gets in touch," Wendy said, "tell him it's urgent."

Jane assured Wendy she would and hung up the phone.

"These are the dates?" Pauline asked, looking over Jane's shoulder at the notepad Jane was studying.

"Yes," Jane said.

"Was there something else?"

"Wendy still wants to speak to Brian," Jane said.

"Why?" Pauline asked, puzzled. "Is there something we don't know about?"

"I don't know," Jane said, "and I didn't like to ask. She's always been sweet on him, but this isn't like that. It's disturbing."

"She sounded threatening when I spoke to her," Pauline said. "Like she'd finally decided Brereton was to blame for Mimi's disappearance."

"She didn't sound threatening this time," Jane said. "She was trying to sound casual, as if it wasn't important, which means it's desperately important."

"Not gin-induced love sickness then," Pauline replied.

"No," Jane said. "I know all Wendy's moods and voices, and this isn't one of them."

Pauline nodded. "Maybe, when we've found Mimi, we'll know if there's more to it."

26

GANGSTERS AT PLAY

THE FOLLOWING MORNING, Ramsay picked up Jane at Pauline's apartment. When Jane exited the apartment, Ramsay laughed.

"Until today, I never knew how much you resembled your sister," he said.

Jane smiled mischievously. "I don't think Pauline has fully understood my disguise yet. I'm not just teasing her; I'm trying to make her see how old she looks to the world." She jumped in the car, and they set out for Corrigan's country home.

"You chose your disguise to tease your sister?" Ramsay asked.

Jane nodded. "Partly, but partly because I think this is what a middle-aged spinster birdwatcher would look like. The two are sort of the same, don't you think?"

Ramsay shook his head. "No, I do not so don't waste your time trying to cause trouble between us. And I thought I said no disguises."

"This isn't a housebreaking disguise," Jane said. "It's a look-nothing-like-Jane-Riddell disguise. I may not know

Corrigan or his people, but they may know me from parties in town."

They were silent for a moment as Jane considered whether he was angry or just amused. Finally, when he didn't elaborate, she continued, "Tell me about this country house."

"It's an old country home of minor gentry, I'd say. It's too far out of town to be a true manor house but not big enough for aristocracy, unless as a shooting lodge."

"There's shooting up on the moors," Jane said thoughtfully. "Has it access to the hilltops?"

"It has and it has small, wooded areas where birds can be shot." His tone was neutral but left no doubt he didn't approve.

"Tosh goes pheasant and grouse shooting in the season," Jane said.

"I've no doubt," Ramsay replied. "That's one gentlemanly pursuit I'm sure they'd all jump at."

"Will we be able to get close to the house," Jane asked, "using the woods as cover, I mean?"

"No. The trees are set in wide, open meadows so you'd be a sitting duck crossing from one to the next," Ramsay said. "When we get there, we'll find a better plan."

"Such as?" Jane asked hopefully. After all, he'd seen the place, he must have an idea.

"I don't know. I wasn't considering creeping up on people who bury their enemies in concrete foundations," Ramsay said.

"They'd have to catch us first," Jane replied.

When they parked on a narrow lane overlooking Corrigan's property, however, she saw Ramsay's point. The house had a wide swathe of lawns and meadows around it and worse, what looked like armed guards looking out from a battlemented roof.

"Can they have armed guards?" Jane asked sulkily. "It seems unfair."

"They can if their guns are licensed," Ramsay said.

"What do you suggest?"

"This morning, we make our way on the roads around the property looking for weak spots that might let us get close. I don't expect Corrigan will be sitting about planning criminal acts to suit our convenience, though."

"All I want to see or hear is Mimi," Jane said. "I don't need anything more criminal than that."

"The grounds are too big for clearly seeing a small poodle," Ramsay replied, as he drove slowly on, occasionally being stopped by farm tractors or flocks of sheep being moved from field to field.

"We could get closer that way," Jane said, as a flock passed across the road in front of them and into one of the fields above Corrigan's house.

"Wearing a sheepskin and on all fours, I presume," Ramsay replied in a satirical tone.

"Why not? I have a sheepskin coat I could wear inside out."

"How long could you wander around on hands and knees in the hard ground out there?" Ramsay asked.

"We've had enough rain lately," Jane said, "the ground will be soft."

"We're still a mile from the house here. We'll keep going."

Their slow progress meant it was an hour before they returned to their original lookout.

"This is the best place," Jane said, "but I don't see how we do it."

"That's what I thought the other day when I visited. To our left, there's a stream running down from the moors, and it has plenty of bushes growing on its banks. That takes us to the first wood, the one immediately below us. After that, we'd need the cover of night."

Jane's face lit up. "Let's do it. Pauline isn't the only one who can sneak up on bad guys."

"Trying to outdo your sister will get you into serious trouble," Ramsay said, locking the car. "We do things because the job needs us to do them, not to score points."

"Do you have a famous older brother?" Jane asked, as they made their way along the lane to where the stream ran under the road.

Ramsay smiled. "I don't, but if I did, I'd still say the same thing."

The hawthorn hedge blocking the entrance from the low bridge was too thick to let them pass. They moved farther along and found a gap in the hedge, which scratched them as they pushed through. Crouching low, they made their way back to the stream with its comforting screen of broom bushes.

"I'm torn to pieces," Jane complained as they wended their way down the hill.

"And you'll be full of bullet holes if you don't keep quiet," Ramsay whispered. "This isn't a game."

As Ramsay had observed, the stream ran into a small, wooded area before disappearing underground. They reached the lower edge of the trees and peered out at the house. A group of men were leaving the door with guns balanced on their forearms, retriever dogs running ahead of them.

Ramsay frowned. "I hope we haven't been spotted," he whispered.

They watched in tense silence as the men began to climb up the slope toward them. A moment before Ramsay was about to say *run!* the men turned left and made their way to another wood.

"Is Corrigan there?" Jane asked.

"I think he's the big one," Ramsay said. "I've only seen him in a business suit so in country tweeds and a hat, I'm not entirely certain."

"I wish we could get closer," Jane grumbled.

"They may yet come this way," Ramsay said. "They'll likely want to shoot birds in this wood too."

"We could be hit," Jane said.

"So long as it's only a flesh wound, and you don't squeal, we'll be fine," Ramsay teased her.

"Very funny," Jane said. "How are we going to get close enough to hear what they're saying?"

"We're not," Ramsay said, "and even if we did, what are the chances of them talking about kidnapped pets. Look at them." He pointed at the group of men making their way purposefully to the other wooded area.

Jane saw what he meant. None of them looked like men who cared about pets. They looked like Corrigan. Men who'd come up through the streets of hard, industrial cities. They'd kick to death the Mimis and Mittens of the world if they saw them.

"Well, someone here must be in charge of the petnapping," Jane said. "There's a Mrs. Corrigan. Maybe she's branching out the family firm from plain old stealing ships' cargoes to pet ransoms. It does have a female touch to it, don't you think?"

Ramsay frowned thoughtfully. "I hadn't thought that but now I see those men, and I know what they do, I see what you mean. Petnapping does have the feminine touch, though I don't see Corrigan letting his wife risk his whole enterprise over something with such a poor reward."

"While those hoodlums are up here shooting pigeons, or whatever they're looking for, why don't we make our way to the house?" Jane asked, ignoring his discouraging comment.

"How?" Ramsay said. "Look at all the open ground between here and the house with lookouts on the roof. Any one of the men shooting birds looks back and we have six men with shotguns on our tail."

"We have to do something!"

"This is why I wanted to escort you today," Ramsay said seriously. "We 'have to' live to tomorrow if we're to put right the wrongs being done. Our being shot and buried on the moors isn't a help to anyone."

Jane fumed, but as she couldn't find a crushing enough response, she said nothing, only stared out at the group of men so intently, she expected them to turn and stare right back.

"After dark is the only hope," Ramsay said, "and I'm betting they let those dogs roam the park to deter trespassers. They look the sort."

Before Jane could answer, a volley of shots rang out and a flock of birds rose from the farther woods, some fell but most flew over the head of the men and landed in the leaf canopy above the heads of Jane and Ramsay.

"We should make our way deeper into the trees," Ramsay said. "When they pick up their victims, they'll come here for another try."

"Birds are even more stupid than I thought," Jane said, following him slowly back the way they'd come while keeping a close watch on the men and dogs. To her horror, a bird that had been struggling began to flutter and fall.

Immediately, a retriever saw the falling bird and raced across the meadow to collect it.

"Hide," whispered Ramsay, and they both crouched down behind stout tree trunks.

Jane heard the dog's arrival outside the wood, heard it bark, the sound of its paws on the ground, then a guttural primitive sound, which she guessed was it picking up the body, and then it was racing back to the men.

"They'll be here soon," Ramsay said. "We must get deeper in, or the dogs will smell or hear us."

Jane found that now she had no wish to argue. The fine line between the dog finding its prey and not finding them had awakened her sense of self-preservation. Ramsay was right. Until this moment, it had been a game to her.

As they retreated, they could no longer see the men and dogs, but they could hear them approaching and Jane's heart began to thump. She was back to the moment she fled her apartment and cold sweat prickled her brow.

"Everybody ready?" she heard a man's voice ask.

"Gimme a minute," another voice, even harder than the first, replied.

"What's the matter with your gun, Tommy?" the first voice asked.

"Dunno. It's not ejecting the cartridge."

"Well sort it out, man," the first voice said, paused and asked, "Are you ready now?"

"Ready."

There was a brief silence before a firecracker explosion among the trees, the whirring of dozens of wings taking flight, and the instantaneous bang of the guns.

"At least you can still shoot straight, Tommy," the first voice said. This time there was some humor in it.

"The birds have settled again," a different voice said.

"Then we should follow them." There was a laugh, followed by, "When I was a kid, pigeon pie was a great treat. Now I feed them to the dogs and pigs."

The voices tailed away as the men left. Ramsay slowly rose, peering through the undergrowth as he did so.

"They're gone," he whispered, "and we should be too."

Ramsay and Jane quickly reached the road while, below them, gunfire continued every few minutes, echoing around the valley, as the men reached new coverts and scared up more targets.

"This investigation's taking too long," Jane said in frustration, as they climbed into the car and Ramsay started the engine. "I don't believe Mimi or Mittens are alive by this point."

Ramsay nodded. "I tend to agree. Still, there's been no bodies dropped on doorsteps, so we must continue."

"Put your foot down," Jane said, her anger forgotten. "I've people to phone and the sooner the better."

Ramsay grinned and pressed his foot on the accelerator.

27

GREAT IDEAS

When Pauline returned from work, she found Jane on the phone and was hastily shushed when she tried to say, 'I'm home.' Seeing Jane wasn't near finishing her conversation, Pauline whispered a quick hello to Inspector Ramsay, who was perched on the arm of the couch looking out of the window, and went to change in her room. When she came out, she saw Jane hang up the handset with a triumphant flourish.

"We had a great idea today," Jane told her excitedly when Pauline entered the living room. Without giving Ramsay a moment to add anything, Jane quickly outlined the idea that Mrs. Corrigan was the pet snatcher and how she, Jane, was going to prove it tomorrow.

"It sounds a lot less lunatic than many of your ideas" Pauline said sarcastically, before adding, "But I'll stay near the office phone tomorrow, in case you discover the whereabouts of the pets, and you need my assistance."

"Of course, I need you," Jane retorted, adding, "I can't rescue a dog and a cat on my own. Mimi doesn't like cats."

"The more I hear of Mimi," Pauline said, "the less I like

her. Shouldn't Inspector Ramsay rescue Mittens? It is his case, after all."

"I'll get Mimi out, you get Mittens," Jane said, "and we'll hand her over to Inspector Ramsay when it's done. He'd be a dead giveaway in a women's salon."

Ramsay laughed and agreed. "By the way, Mal the Magician has had a reminder. The kidnapper now wants eleven thousand pounds and says the price will go up a thousand a week until it reaches fifteen thousand. At that point they will kill the cat."

"They?"

"That's what the voice said."

"Man or woman?" Pauline asked.

"A man and it was a trunk call."

"It could still be Brereton then, calling from London or Birmingham," Pauline said.

"I thought that too," Ramsay answered, "but if it is, I still think the pets are being held locally. This is where I'm hoping Jane learns something new for us."

"I know where Mrs. Corrigan gets her hair permed and her nails polished," Jane said, bursting in on the conversation, determined to share her success. "She has an appointment tomorrow and so do I!" The expressions of her two companions were sufficient reward.

"That's excellent work, Jane. It can't be soon enough," Ramsay said, genuinely impressed. "I didn't set much store by this theory at first but I'm coming round to it. Even if the woman is innocent, someone on the Corrigan side of the turf war may know enough about it to be useful to us."

"Tosh's embarrassment at having his wife's pet stolen would be a great source of amusement in the Corrigan camp, don't you think?" Pauline asked.

"I do. Even if they aren't behind it, someone may have

shared it with the Corrigans to gain favor," Ramsay said, rising and putting on his hat and jacket.

"Tomorrow, we'll learn everything there is to know," Pauline replied, smiling mischievously at Jane as she escorted Ramsay to the door.

"He thinks there may be something in it now," Jane grumbled when Pauline closed the door behind Ramsay. "He was pretty negative earlier."

"Maybe he was just being cautious but the point about using Tosh's embarrassment when you're talking with Mrs. Corrigan is a good one, Jane."

"You two still think Brereton is behind the Mittens snatch," Jane said, her mind already jumping to a different train of thought.

"The coincidence of the cars, his and the one in the lane that night being the same make and color, is too strong," Pauline said. "Somehow, he has to be, even if he isn't behind Mimi's disappearance."

"Maybe I should phone Wendy," Jane said, thoughtfully. "If Magic Mal has been contacted again, maybe Wendy has."

Pauline nodded. "Go ahead. Just don't give away where you're staying."

As Jane replaced the handset after talking to Wendy, she said, "Tosh has told her to forget Mimi and buy a new dog."

"Poor Wendy," Pauline said sympathetically. She could remember her own feelings whenever one of the dogs or cats on the farm died or disappeared during her childhood.

"Tosh says she must get a dog that can look after itself. One that will savage anyone who tries to walk off with it," Jane continued. "That won't do for Wendy. She wants one she can baby."

"Ugh," Pauline replied. She continued after a brief pause. "You asked Wendy if there was something else wrong. What did she say?"

"She said if I find Mimi, she'll explain."

"If it's bothering her when she's this upset over Mimi, it must be serious," Pauline said.

"Oh, Wendy's a worrier," Jane replied. "It's probably nothing."

Pauline nodded. "Well, for now, your meeting with Mrs. Corrigan tomorrow, if it happens, is our best hope for a new lead."

"It will happen," Jane said. "I have this, Pauline."

"Be sure she doesn't smell a rat, or you'll have a second gangster on your tail," Pauline cautioned her.

28

RAMSAY FINDS THE CAR

Ramsay had only just stepped out of his car in the B&B driveway when Bracken nudged his knee. They hadn't been anywhere interesting since the morning walk and that was hours ago.

Ramsay grinned. "You're right, Bracken" he said. "We both need fresh air and sunshine."

He grabbed hat, jacket, and leash. Clipping the leash to Bracken's collar they left the B&B and headed out on the streets they'd come to know so well.

"We'll come back by Clifton Manor," Ramsay said, as they began walking. "I may step in and talk again to the old lady."

Bracken ignored him sulkily. The route they were taking was heading into the village and away from the fields, woods, and rabbit warrens he particularly loved. Lampposts, corners, and other dog trail markers were only interesting when you knew the other dogs. He knew no one here and consequently, the scents were tantalizing, promising even, without ever fulfilling the promise.

He perked up when they turned off the street down a

lane leading to the fields, and to show his appreciation, sniffed a trail to the door he knew Ramsay was interested in.

"You're right, Bracken. That's the janitor's house and I'm sure he was the one who got Mittens out of the home that night, but we've looked there many times now and there's no cat to be seen."

His duty done; Bracken continued down the lane to where the rabbits lived. Unfortunately, there were sheep in the field and Ramsay wouldn't let him off the leash, so his sulkiness returned.

"It's no good looking at me like that," Ramsay said to him as they continued along the lane, climbing to the top of a low hilltop covered in trees that were suitably spaced to give a view over the village.

Ramsay was pleased when he reached the summit because he remembered that only days ago climbing here had him out of breath. Today it didn't. Now he no longer had a desk to sit at, nor a cafeteria to snack at, the result was a slowly improving Ramsay.

He gazed out over the village, looking sleepy in the late summer afternoon sun, and noticed it was visiting time at Clifton Manor. Three cars were parked in the forecourt and another two were parked in the lane beside it. His eyes continued picking out landmarks, the church and the pub, the smoky haze of Salford and Manchester to the south, and finally, the B&B with his car parked outside.

Maybe it was the sight of his car, so easily recognized as a Ford Popular, that started it, but his eyes returned quickly to Clifton Manor and the cars outside, particularly the two in the lane. One was lighter, cream colored maybe, but the other looked like the car he now knew was an Austin Westminster. And it was a dark color, just like Brereton's.

"Come on Bracken," he said, tugging at the leash, "we have to go."

Going down was a lot quicker than climbing up and Ramsay and Bracken flew over the ground, much to Bracken's delight. This was more like it.

Agonizing that the car would be gone before he could get there kept Ramsay trotting even when they reached level ground. It was a huge relief when he turned into the lane and saw the car still parked.

"Try and look innocent, Bracken," Ramsay said. "Just as if we're on our afternoon stroll and not interested in that car at all."

Bracken had no interest in cars so he wouldn't have given the game away, but Ramsay couldn't take his eyes off it. An Austin Westminster, dark maroon, with the local plates that had led them first to Brereton. Except, this wasn't Brereton's car. He'd followed that car long enough to know its plate number by heart.

"I think we have our catnapper, Bracken," he said. "We'll call in on Adie and see how she's getting along."

Ramsay was welcomed by Nurse Carey, who'd let him in on his first visit and who he'd followed to eliminate her from his enquiries.

"Mr. Ramsay. How nice to see you again and Bracken, too. Adie doesn't have a visitor today, so she'll be pleased to see the two of you, I'm sure."

As she led him through the building, Ramsay asked, "Do you know the owner of the Austin Westminster outside?" They'd already slipped up over one Westminster and he didn't want a second.

"That's Mr. Aymes' son's car, why?"

"I'm looking to change my car and I've been thinking the Westminster has what I'm looking for, now I'm a retired man of leisure." He laughed. "I thought I might ask his opinion of the car."

"Well, he's in his father's room right now but I could ask him to find you and talk, if he's a mind to."

"Thank you, that would be helpful," Ramsay said. They found Adie sitting outside enjoying the warm afternoon. "Hello, Adie, remember me?"

"Have you found Mittens?"

"Not yet," Ramsay said, "but I think I'm very close now."

"Then you should be finding Mittens and not visiting me. Malcom is growing frantic. He can't raise anything like the money they're asking, and the television people want Malcom and Mittens to start rehearsing next week."

Ramsay was about to reply when a middle-aged man entered, smartly dressed and groomed. His thinning hair was slicked and glossy with Brylcreem. He approached and asked, "Mr. Ramsay?"

Ramsay rose, extending his hand. "That's me. You must be Mr. Aymes' son." The man's shiny hair and too white teeth gave him a predatory appearance, like a shark just out of the water.

"That's right, Ronnie Aymes," the man said. "The nurse said you wanted to know about the Westminster."

"My old Ford Pop is on its last legs," Ramsay said, grinning, "and I've a mind for something a bit more luxurious. What's the Westminster like to drive?"

"Lovely car," Ronnie said. "And, yes, comfortable seats and cab with room for a whole family."

"You've had no trouble with it?"

"None at all," Ronnie said. "Two years I've had it and nowhere near a garage except for servicing. I'd recommend it to anyone."

"Thanks," Ramsay said, smiling. "Having an owner's

perspective is so much better than the motoring press or the dealer's view, I always think."

"You're right there," Aymes began when his eye was caught by a woman waving impatiently from the hall. "Well, I must go, or I'll never hear the end of it from the missus. It was nice to meet you." He nodded and followed his wife who was already at the front door.

"Old Mr. Aymes never liked Mittens," Adie said.

"From what I've been told," Ramsay replied, "hardly anyone did."

"Mebbe but he was the worst," Adie said.

"In what way was he the worst?"

"Once, he tried to hit Mittens with his walking stick. And his cursing... well, I never heard the like of it," Adie said, "and I've lived on farms all my life."

Smiling at this tale of wrongdoing, Ramsay wrote down Ronnie's name beside the Westminster's number in his notebook and settled to coaxing Adie into a better frame of mind.

An hour later, he was in the telephone box and on the phone to Logan asking for an address for Ronnie Aymes.

"You do know the police can't hand this kind of information out to the public," Logan reminded him.

"If I were just a member of the public, I'd agree. But I'm not. Be quick though, Mittens has a rehearsal soon and I need to get her there."

Logan laughed. "If this comes off, even I'll watch the show, so I know why there's all this fuss over a cat."

"Mittens, as I told you, is a star of stage and radio and not just a cat."

"I still don't know how that radio thing works," Logan said. "Maybe if I had youngsters, I would."

Ramsay thanked him and hung up. "Come on, Bracken.

Now we can finish our walk that was so wonderfully interrupted by my superior detective skills."

As in Bracken's opinion Ramsay missed every one of the clues they walked past every day, Bracken diplomatically said nothing.

However, they hadn't gone very far when Ramsay realized he was going to need a better description and photo of Mittens.

"We have to go back the way we came, Bracken," he said. "When I see Mittens in Mr. Aymes' house, I want to be sure it's her and not another cat with two white paws."

Returning to the phone box they'd just left, he phoned Magic Mal and was promised a publicity photo, larger than the picture he had, and was told how to make Mittens do her most famous trick of rolling over when given triggering words.

"Bring the photo around to Clifton Manor tonight," Ramsay said. "We'll meet outside, and you can train me on using the magic words." They agreed a time and Ramsay hung up the phone.

"This time we can go, Bracken," he said brightly. Bracken's expression suggested this time he was not going to be so easily won over.

29

ANOTHER GREAT IDEA

JANE WATCHED the hair salon from the café across the street. She'd taken an early bus into town because she wanted to be sure of seeing Mrs. Corrigan arrive; now she was wishing she hadn't. All the tea she'd drunk was urging her to leave the window for a comfort break. She rose, but seeing a Daimler car arriving opposite, sat down again, all thought of comfort forgotten.

The chauffeur who opened the door for Mrs. Corrigan looked like he'd been a heavyweight boxer at some time in his life. Sean meant to keep his wife safe even at the hairdressers, Jane thought with a wry smile.

She quickly paid her bill and exited the café, hurrying across the street so as not to miss a moment of the time Mrs. Corrigan was inside. Her own appointment wasn't for another fifteen minutes, which was the best she could get on the afternoon before but arriving early might get her into the chair next to her target.

It did, though not right away. She had time to 'powder her nose' before being escorted to a chair near Mrs. Corrigan. She wanted close enough to talk quietly but beggars can't be choosers, so she smiled at the woman between them and said hello.

As the washing, cutting, styling, and curling processes moved slowly on, she was pleased the conversation she'd started became amicable and included everyone. It had happened naturally and without her forcing it at all. She steered the conversation from boyfriends, husbands, and lovers to pets. That too promoted lively discussion, though not yet of the kind Jane wanted.

Deciding to force the pace, Jane asked, "Have you heard of these pet snatches that are going on?" She watched her companions carefully for their reactions.

Neither of the two women claimed knowledge of such wicked crimes and asked what she'd heard.

"I know of two people who've had their pets taken and received ransom demands," Jane said. "One for a cat, and the other a dog." Again, she looked for a flicker of recognition in the faces of the two women but there was none. Frustrated, she became more daring. "Both animals are worth a lot of money," she continued. "You can't trust anyone these days, can you?"

Everyone agreed times were shockingly bad but still there was no sign of Mrs. Corrigan being anything but mildly interested.

"You said you had dogs, I think, Doreen," Jane said, addressing Mrs. Corrigan directly. "You might want to take extra care for the next little while."

"I will," Mrs. Corrigan replied placidly. "That's good to know. I'll make sure my husband knows too. He's more on the security side of the property than I am. We live out in the country, so trespassers are a constant nuisance. He's fired a shotgun over the heads of some of them. People have no respect for property. They think the countryside belongs to everyone and can't understand it's fields and farms."

"What do you farm?" Jane asked. "I grew up on a farm. Then dad died and we had to leave."

"We fatten cattle for other farmers and rent out most of the land to surrounding farms," Doreen said. "But we have plenty of animals about the place."

"We used to have dogs for herding the sheep and cows," Jane said. "They were always good for playing games with us children when they weren't working."

"Ours are mainly pointers and retrievers," Doreen said. "We have shooting parties in the season."

"Do you have pets as well?"

"I do but my husband doesn't care for pets, though he likes his dogs well enough. I have spaniels, and like the queen, I have two Welsh corgis."

"No poodles then," Jane said, laughing to show what she thought of such fluffy bundles.

"Heavens no," Doreen replied. "We think meanly of people who have such things." She smiled to show she was joking. Jane wondered if it was a sly dig at Wendy McIntosh.

"Not real dogs, I agree," Jane said, still laughing. "But what I said earlier is worth thinking about. The pet thefts I mean. Your dogs may be safe at your country property but the thefts I know of took place close to or in town."

Doreen smiled. "We have good security in town, have no fear of that." There was a quality in her tone that suggested more than just an alarm wired to the doors and windows.

"That's good," Jane said. "I don't have pets myself, so it isn't a problem but every time I hear someone talking about theirs, the story comes back to me, and I share it. It may not even be true; you know how these urban legends get around."

There was silence as the hairdressers fiddled with rollers on the three women's heads, which left Jane time to consider whether she'd learned anything. She'd neither seen nor heard signs in Doreen's expression or voice to suggest she had a part in the pet thefts. Was she just a good actress? She looked shrewd enough to be careful not to let slip any hint of wrongdoing; maybe that came with the company she kept. And she may well know that if she didn't keep secrets, her husband might well have *her* buried out on the moors. On balance, Jane felt she'd gained nothing. Should she ramp up her interrogation or would that be too dangerous? Pauline was right about not wanting two gangsters on her tail.

When the hair of each was safely enclosed in the driers, the hairdressers left. Sylvie, the woman between Jane and Doreen said, "Are these pet thefts for big sums of money? I have a cat and I'd hate to lose her. She's everything to me but my Ralph wouldn't spend a penny to get her back if she were taken. I'd have to find the money myself."

"They're both for more than ten thousand pounds, I hear," Jane said.

"How much?" Sylvie cried.

Jane nodded. "It's not cheap, so keep your cat safe is my advice."

"That's madness," Sylvie replied. "I couldn't raise that much on my own."

"The kidnappers would likely assume your husband would fork out for your sake, if not the cat's."

"Well, he wouldn't," Sylvie says. "She makes him sneeze."

Jane laughed. "Then don't tell him what I've told you or he may kidnap the cat and blame it on the pet snatchers."

"That's true," Sylvie said, even more earnestly that she'd

spoken before. "I hope he doesn't hear of it from someone else."

"Ten thousand is a lot of money for a pet," Doreen said slowly. "These must be rich owners."

"Well, one is, I hear," Jane said. "Sadly, the other isn't. So his cat, unlike the cat in the song, will not come back."

"That's sad," Sylvie said. "He can get another, surely."

"I'm sure he will," Jane said, watching Doreen from the corner of her eye. Something was in Doreen's mind, but what?

"You seem puzzled, Doreen," Jane said.

"When you first mentioned it, I thought we were talking the stuff that happened in our neighborhood when we were kids, and I knew we were safe from greedy or vicious youngsters. What you've just said is different though, isn't it?"

Jane nodded. Now she had Doreen's attention. "It's quite out of the usual, which is why we aren't hearing much about it. No one wants to start copycats on something like this."

"No, indeed," Doreen said. "I can't imagine anyone paying out that much for a pet. You could buy a herd of cattle for that. It can't be right."

"As I said, you know how stories get around and they grow in the telling," Jane said. Was Doreen only hearing this for the first time? Her expression suggested real concern now, which it hadn't done before.

Sylvie added, "Unless the owners are fabulously rich, pop stars and the like. I can imagine a millionaire paying out for a favorite pet," she laughed, "or more likely a wife's favorite pet."

"Yes," Doreen said, still thinking things through, before adding with a rueful smile, "or his mistress's pet."

Jane's heart sank as she realized the pet thief wasn't Mrs. Corrigan but Mr. Corrigan's mistress. Who was she? Who could Jane ask? With this new revelation, Jane found an overwhelming desire to be away. Mrs. Corrigan could no longer hold her interest as her mind raced through all the people she knew who might know of Mr. Corrigan's mistress.

Sylvie laughed. "You're right. Thankfully, me and Ralph aren't rich enough for pet nappers to target."

"Me neither," Jane said, absentmindedly, still deciding on who to contact for information.

"And we have good security," Doreen said, "so we're all safe." Her expression, however, suggested she thought otherwise.

"Speaking of pop stars," Sylvie said, "did you read that story in the Sunday papers the other day?"

Jane sighed with relief. Now she was convinced Doreen wasn't the petnapper, she was happy to have the conversation take a different turn. As the pop star was London-based, she had no personal knowledge of them and could cheerfully 'tut-tut' with the others. By the time their hair was dry, the three women were talked out on all the latest society gossip, and they went their separate ways amicably without any inclination to ever see each other again.

30

RAMSAY AND MITTENS

THAT EVENING, Ramsay and Bracken were patiently waiting outside Clifton Manor Residential Home, Ramsay hoping Magic Mal wouldn't be late. Heaven knew what the residents of the home would think if they were watching him pace up and down the lane. Mal, however, arrived on time and handed over a large 6" by 8" black and white photo with Mittens' name and pawprint in the lower right corner. He pointed out small details in coloring around the ears that would definitively identify her and then walked Ramsay through the process that would set up the trick. He showed Ramsay the movements he needed to do, the words Ramsay had to say, and the treats that would be expected once the trick was performed.

"Show her you have those before you start," Mal said. "She can be difficult if she isn't certain there's a treat at the end. It really would be better if I came with you, you know," Mal added anxiously.

Ramsay shook his head. "If I must break into a property to rescue Mittens, it's better only one of us is involved. I'll phone the moment I have her and then you can meet me

Miss Riddell and the Pet Thefts

and confirm I have Mittens. If it's the wrong cat, I'll take it back without anyone being the wiser."

His preparations made, Ramsay returned to the B&B hoping Logan would phone tonight or early next day at the latest.

RAMSAY AND BRACKEN returned from their outing and he was enjoying morning tea with the B&B owner, when the phone rang. The landlady snatched it up, only to hand it to him. Her disappointed expression suggested she too was waiting for an important call.

"Here's the address," Logan said. "Not so far from where you are, I think."

"Thanks. I owe you another bottle," Ramsay said.

"We're approaching a case rather than a single bottle," Logan retorted. "Just make sure you don't do anything stupid with this. I won't save you if you do, no matter how much whisky you offer."

Ramsay assured him he would be a model citizen and not cause trouble for his old colleague and returned to finish his tea.

"I must go out," he told his landlady. "Could you look after Bracken again this morning, please."

"I should add dog sitting fees onto my rent," she replied smiling. "But he's no trouble and I enjoy the company so this time, I won't charge you." Bracken rubbed her hand with his nose.

RAMSAY DROVE around the streets that bordered Aymes' new suburban house until he had the lay of the land. It was quiet. The men of the houses were at work, women were indoors working or out shopping. It was a normal day in the suburbs. He parked and walked to the address he'd been given, keeping a wide view of the streets and garden in case someone appeared. No one did. The bay window that faced the street showed nobody moving inside the house and, sadly, no cat on the sill. However, this was the shady side of the house. The morning sun was on the back, the south side. That's where a cat would sit.

Ramsay strolled to the corner of the property and turned into the lane between the Aymes' house and its neighbor. The windows here were frosted glass, clearly the toilet. He moved on until he saw the kitchen window. And Mittens, sunning herself behind the glass. At least, it looked like Mittens. Now all he had to do was get her out, study her closely, and test her response to the trick instructions.

Luck was on the side of the law today, Ramsay thought as he entered the garden. Seeing nobody through the kitchen window, he showed Mittens the treat to hold her attention while he slid his penknife blade between the window and frame to lift the catch. It was the work of a minute and Mittens stepped out into his arms expecting her treat.

Ramsay placed her on the ground and went through the words and movements. For a second, he thought he'd done it wrong, but she rolled over, stood up, and meowed in a way that left him in no doubt she expected to be paid. He held the treat for her to take and scooped her up in his arms again when she snatched at it.

Pushing the window shut, he quickly walked back to his car and, with Mittens on the passenger seat, drove back to the B&B. He felt elated and found himself trembling. Whether that was excitement, trepidation, or a guilty conscience over housebreaking, he couldn't tell.

Ramsay's phone call to Magic Mal had the entertainer at Clifton Manor in record time.

"I hope you'll tell the police and have the thieves arrested," Mal said, when he'd finally convinced himself that Mittens was real.

"I can't now I've taken the cat," Ramsay said apologetically. "She was the only evidence of the thief. It's best you take Mittens back to your home and both of you go off to rehearsals without saying a word to anyone about this."

"Who did have her?"

"That needn't concern you if you keep her close until you leave. You have your co-star and fame is calling you," Ramsay said. "The wonderful new world of television beckons, so get away and don't look back."

"It's not right," Mal grumbled. Then he nodded and said, "Still, it's good advice. I'll leave for London in the morning. Mittens and I can put it out of our minds."

"I'll look for the show when it gets broadcast," Ramsay said, shaking Mal's hand. "Now, let's you and I say our farewells to Adie, and I can say goodbye to my part in this unpleasantness."

Adie's reaction to the good news of Mittens' return was much as Ramsay had imagined it would be. Grudgingly gratified for Ramsay's success, while demanding he not overcharge on his expenses, before crossly scolding Mal to take better care of his pet in the future because she couldn't be expected to do it again, not after this experience.

Ramsay assured her he'd charge only for expenses beyond his living costs and wished Mal goodbye. He promised to call in on Adie the following day with his bill. When she'd warned him about overcharging, he'd almost told her he wouldn't accept a penny but his native commonsense prevailed; the B&B costs were too much to be ignored.

In future, however, he wouldn't do any investigations that meant charging elderly people such expensive costs.

* * *

While Ramsay was returning Mittens to her owner, Jane was back at Pauline's apartment and searching through her diary for the phone numbers of those she thought might know who Corrigan's mistress might be. This meant connecting with people who'd missed her presence at recent events, so she had a lot of catching up to do and she was still working on finding the mysterious mistress when Pauline came home.

"Are you sure she said he had a mistress?" Pauline asked, when Jane explained her search.

"As good as," Jane said. "It was more the way she said it, rather than what she said."

"But it's a joke anyone might make," Pauline said, when Jane recounted the conversation, "particularly a wife of many years who feels her powers of persuasion diminishing."

"I know what I heard," Jane said, dialing the next number.

"I hope you're paying for all these calls," Pauline said, imagining the monthly phone bill.

"We'll pay it out of our fee," Jane said, holding her hand over the mouthpiece waiting for the number to pick up.

"What fee?" Pauline said. "Nobody asked us to find their pets. Only Inspector Ramsay might get something."

"Wendy will see us right," Jane said, before the phone was connected. "Hello, Magsy," she said, waving Pauline away.

. . .

"Well?" Pauline asked, when Jane hung up.

"Nobody knows for sure," Jane said, "but they think he spends a lot of time with his secretary."

Pauline frowned. "The same could be said about me or any woman in a position that brings her into contact with men who work all the hours of the day. It doesn't mean anything."

"Well, at least I'm turning up possible leads," Jane replied hotly. "What have you done?"

"I'm working eight-to-five and more," Pauline said, "which doesn't leave a lot of time for wild goose chases."

"I want to see this secretary," Jane said. "We could watch her enter and leave work tomorrow."

"You mean Corrigan's place at the docks?" Pauline asked.

"Yes."

"A car with two women in it sitting outside their door would look out of place," Pauline said.

"Then we dress as cleaners or something and find somewhere to watch from," Jane said. "We have to do something."

"We have no reason to suppose she's his mistress, let alone that she's stealing pets," Pauline said.

"Fine. I'll go alone."

"Get Inspector Ramsay to accompany you," Pauline said. "He has spare time, and a man won't look so out-of-place at the docks."

"He'll take the credit for the work I'm doing," Jane said, miffed.

"Even if he did," Pauline replied, "you know I'm right. I'll phone him now."

. . .

Ramsay was quickly brought to the B&B's phone, and he agreed that Pauline's concern made a lot of sense and Pauline handed the phone over to Jane.

"You're willing to join me, Inspector?" Jane asked.

"I am. You're getting good information," he said, then added, "We need to be at the docks by seven, to be sure of catching them arriving at work."

"Do we?" Jane asked.

Ramsay laughed. "Docks work industrial hours. I'll pick you up at 6:30 am. Don't keep me waiting."

"But Corrigan and the others won't keep those hours," Jane protested. "He has to drive in from the country."

"Even if he doesn't keep those hours himself, he'll expect his people to be there when shipments arrive." Ramsay paused, savoring the moment. "Oh. I have some news you and your sister may be interested in," he added casually.

"What's that?" Jane asked. She could hear the amusement in his voice.

"Just that I found, and returned, Mittens to Magic Mal." Ramsay grinned at Jane's gasp of surprise and Pauline asking what Ramsay had said. He heard Jane explain before Pauline came to the phone.

"Where?" Pauline asked.

"At a house not ten miles away from the residential home," Ramsay said. "There's no petnapping ring, no Mr. Big here. Just a spiteful old man and a son without a conscience who wanted cash."

"Are you certain?" Pauline demanded. "You've interviewed the kidnapper and you're certain?"

"I haven't," Ramsay said. "I just took Mittens back to her owner and told them to get out of town."

"Who had Mittens?" Pauline asked. "One of the staff?"

"No. One of the residents' son," Ramsay said. "I'm pretty

sure it went like this: The cat hated the resident who hated her in turn. He told his son to take it out of the home."

"But he couldn't just walk out with it," Pauline objected.

"I suspect he paid the janitor to take it at the end of his shift. They made the handover of cash and cat in the lane, which is how the car was seen."

"At least he didn't kill Mittens," Pauline said.

"He was probably supposed to. But hearing from everyone in the home that Mittens was a star, he decided to try for some cash, which was a mistake because it brought about my investigation. If he'd killed Mittens or asked a price Mal could pay, everything would have been fine. But like many people, he imagined entertainers on television were all paid beyond our wildest dreams."

"So, everything was just at and around the residential home," Pauline said, disappointed.

"Yes, I'm certain now there's no connection to Mimi's disappearance."

"There must be," Pauline replied. "The coincidence is too great."

"Then the connection lies elsewhere," Ramsay said. "It isn't in the actual stealing."

Pauline thought quickly. "Has Mal left already?"

"No, tomorrow morning he said."

"Phone him and ask who books his club tours," Pauline said. "Quickly!"

"I'll phone back," Ramsay said and hung up.

"I told you who manages Mal's bookings," Jane said indignantly. "Don't you remember?"

"I want to be sure," Pauline said. "Your party friend Lance may boast about booking acts he doesn't have."

31

MIMI IS RESCUED

Ramsay retrieved Mal's number from his notebook and dialed. The phone rang and rang until he was about to give up when it was answered.

"Hello?"

"It's me, Ramsay. Who's the impresario who books your club tours in the North?"

"He calls himself Lance Delaval," Mal replied, "though I suspect it's not his real name."

"Where can I find him?"

"He has offices on Deansgate," Mal said. "Look for Delaval Theatrical Agency in the telephone book. What's this about? You think he was involved in stealing Mittens?"

"Not at all," Ramsay said. "It's a completely different matter I'm looking into that also has an entertainment side to it. Thanks for your help." He hung up and dialed Pauline's number.

"Inspector?" Pauline said, as she snatched up the phone's handset.

"Lance Delaval," Ramsay said. "Now we need Jane to tell us all about him. I'm sure she'll know."

Jane who was listening nodded. "I told you both at the start," she said, crossly, "but you didn't listen. Anyway, now you *are* interested, he's an old letch but every entertainer up here in the North needs to be on his good side, or they don't get bookings."

"Has he been to your apartment?" Pauline asked.

"Of course he has. He's at all the parties and he's good fun," Jane replied. "At least, he is when he's high, which is most of the time. You think he has Mimi? Why would he?"

"I think he heard about Mittens from Mal and saw his chance for easy money," Pauline said.

Jane was about to protest but stopped herself. "There are rumors," she began.

"About?" Ramsay shouted down the phone, frustrated at the slow way this information was dribbling out.

"About him being in financial trouble," Jane said. "He gambles and likes all the latest drug crazes and there are whispers he owes money."

"If he owes money to gambling syndicates or drug dealers, he might be willing to risk your friend Tosh's wrath," Pauline suggested.

"He wouldn't hurt Mimi though," Jane said. "He and Wendy are good friends."

"I hardly like to ask," Pauline said, "but how good of friends are they?"

"Nothing like you're suggesting," Jane said, flushing red.

"You do see what Pauline's getting at though, don't you?" Ramsay asked.

"Even if there was something between them, Wendy wouldn't take part in stealing Mimi," Jane said. "If Lance snatched Mimi, he did it alone."

"Where does he live?" Pauline asked.

"He lives with his wife in Cheshire, where all the rich

live, but he stays mainly in his penthouse apartment in town," Jane said. "We could go there now. He'll be out for sure. He's never at home."

"What say you, Inspector?" Pauline asked.

"I'm with Jane on this. I'll be at your flat in thirty minutes or thereabouts."

From her apartment window, Pauline and Jane saw Ramsay's car parking and were outside when he arrived at the building.

"Which of our cars is the best get-away vehicle?" Ramsay asked, grinning.

"Mine's newer than yours, Inspector," Pauline said, "and mine has four doors, which would make for a quicker getaway than one of us having to climb in the back seat of your old Popular. I suggest we use mine."

With that agreed, they set off for the center of Manchester where they ran into a snag. Jane had been to Delaval's apartment more than once, she claimed, but couldn't show them where it was.

"I don't drive there," Jane protested, when Pauline said she *must* know.

"Then how do you get there?"

"People drive, I don't," Jane said. "And they're parties, no one can remember where they've been after a party, can they?"

Pauline assured her sister that every party she'd been to, she most certainly *could* remember where she'd been.

"Then it wasn't much of a party," Jane snapped back, then shouted. "Stop!"

Pauline braked sharply and pulled the car over to the roadside. "Well?"

"That church is near his place," Jane said, pointing at an ornate red brick building.

"This isn't far from his office and the theater," Ramsay said, "so it makes sense. Let's get out and walk. Jane might recognize more if we're walking."

Pauline parked off the street and they returned to the church where Jane looked about her, frowning in concentration.

Pauline gritted her teeth. She very much wanted Jane to hurry for it was growing dark in the streets between the buildings and she was never comfortable in big cities. However, she knew the more she pestered Jane, the less connections to the buildings her sister would make.

"There," Jane said, triumphantly. "That's the building." She pointed to an old Victorian block of apartments that still had an air of gentility to it, unlike so many others where the city's decline was creeping over them.

Crossing the street, they found the entrance and read the names on the bell buttons.

"Told you," Jane crowed, delighted to be right. She pressed the bell and waited. After minutes had passed without a reply, she pressed it again.

"And I told you he'd be out," she said, when again there was no reply.

"Then how do we get in?" Ramsay asked.

"There's a fire escape at the back of the building," Jane replied. "I've used it many times to get away when things got out of hand."

"Charming," Pauline said sarcastically.

Jane led them around to a wrought iron stair with gate and railings leading up to the top floor.

"Is the gate locked?" Pauline asked.

"Of course," Jane said, "but it's easy to climb over."

"Then I don't see the point of the gate," Pauline replied.

Jane sighed. "Gates and locks are only to keep out honest people. Surely, a great detective like you should have realized that by now."

Ramsay decided he'd intervene before the sniping got out of hand. "You two return to the front door. I'll climb up. If there's no one there, I'll break in and open the downstairs door when you ring the bell. That way we can search the place properly for clues about Mimi."

"You don't think she'll be here?" Pauline asked.

"If he isn't here often enough to feed and walk the dog, he'll have found a safer spot for her," Ramsay replied. "But there'll be an address inside somewhere. Now go." He waited until they'd rounded the corner of the building and were out of sight before hitching himself up and over the gate. The fewer witnesses of his breaking into locked places, the better.

At the top of the stairs, he peered into the darkened room, a kitchen with pans and dishes piled high in the sink. He suspected Mr. Delaval could no longer pay for a maid service. Clearly, his wife didn't stay here when she was in town.

The door latch was child's play with his range of skeleton keys, the long-ago confiscated property of a burglar. Ramsay had brought them with him into retirement. Inside, the room smelled of dirty dishes and worse. He hoped he wasn't going to find a body, Delaval's or Mimi's.

Groping for a switch, he found one and turned on the light. The kitchen was as disgusting as it smelled. He crossed the floor, noting two empty dog bowls on the tiled floor. Mimi?

He found the light switch for the main room of the

apartment and switched it on. A pathetic sight greeted his eyes. The inert form of a small, white poodle lay on a couch. The doorbell rang and he ran to press the buzzer and let the Riddell sisters into the building. Jane, he was sure, would be devastated.

Ramsay made his way back to the dog and his heart leapt. It tried valiantly to raise its head but couldn't. He rushed to the kitchen, filled a bowl with water, and brought it back, placing it beside the dog's head, which he lifted so it could lap the water. No sooner had the dog begun tasting the water when the apartment's doorbell rang, and Ramsay had to lower its head to go and open the door.

"Come in," he said brusquely to Pauline and Jane. "We have an emergency." Hurrying back to the dog, he once again lifted its head to drink.

Slowly, with each splash of water, the dog began to revive. "It is Mimi, isn't it?" Ramsay asked Jane.

She nodded, tears in her eyes. "Who would leave an animal to die like this?"

"One of your friends," Pauline said, as saddened as Jane but furious too, "or maybe that should be fiends."

"He's probably lying comatose somewhere," Ramsay said, pointing to the drug paraphernalia on the nearby table. "You may want to check the other rooms."

Pauline went to do that while Jane took over tending to Mimi from Ramsay, who left to join Pauline in her search.

After Pauline and Ramsay had searched each room, they returned to the living room where Mimi was now sitting up.

"He isn't here," Ramsay said, stroking Mimi's head, "but we shouldn't stay too long. In case he, or his wife, returns."

Jane shook her head. "Hannah doesn't come here. They practically live separate lives these days."

Ramsay's gaze swept slowly around the room. "I can see why she doesn't."

"It wasn't always like this," Jane said, irritated by the criticism directed at one of her friends.

"We still should leave," Ramsay said. "The neighbors may know he's away, and hearing us, call the police."

"They didn't hear Mimi these past days," Jane replied, stroking the dog.

"There may be dog food in the fridge," Pauline said. "She'll be stronger with something inside her." She opened the fridge and found a half full can of food.

"Not too much to eat," Ramsay warned. "We don't want her throwing up all over us while we're driving home."

"I'll take her round to Wendy tomorrow," Jane said, while Mimi was gulping down the food placed in her bowl.

"No," Pauline said. "If you take her back, Tosh will be even more convinced it was you who stole her. Inspector Ramsay must do that. Does her collar still have Wendy's phone number on it?"

A quick check showed it did.

"Then tomorrow, Inspector Ramsay phones and tells Wendy that Mimi has been discovered in a lock-up with a number of other pets and she can collect her somewhere that doesn't point to you or me."

"Tosh may still think I was to blame," Jane objected.

"Then we need something that shows you aren't," Pauline said. "You know them. What would convince them?"

"I don't know," Jane said.

"Then you'd better be part of the investigation," Ramsay said. "Phone her tomorrow after Mimi is returned and tell her how you worked with me to find Mimi. Lay it on thick, lots of difficulty, lots of hard work, much danger but you did it."

Jane thought for a moment and shook her head. "We all hand Mimi over together. I'll say I brought in both of you to help me find Mimi and we can describe what we did. Three witness statements must be better than one or two."

Pauline and Ramsay exchanged glances before Pauline said, "If you think that will persuade them, let's do it."

32

THE CASE CONTINUES WITHOUT PAULINE

NEXT MORNING, when Jane was confident Tosh would be at his office, she phoned Wendy. Hearing Wendy's voice, Jane said, "It's me, Jane. I have good news."

"You have Mimi?"

"We've rescued her," Jane replied. "We'd like to hand her over but, as things stand, me going anywhere near your place might be," she hesitated, "well, uncomfortable, let's say."

"I can meet you."

"Without the usual driver you have?" Jane asked.

"He can't follow me into women's places." Wendy laughed.

"Book a nail or hair appointment today and tell me where to be. I'll deliver Mimi through the back door of the salon." Jane rang off and glanced at Ramsay who was waiting with her to make the exchange.

Jane said to Ramsay, "I'm not going to mention Lance, when we talk to her. I hope you won't either. I don't want anyone killed over this."

Ramsay stroked Mimi's head and then Bracken's ears to

prevent either becoming jealous. "I still see this fine dog," he patted Mimi as he spoke, "lying on that couch. I thought she was dead. Six months ago, I would have been sad but no more than that. Now I have Bracken, my feelings toward people who abuse animals has changed a lot."

"Still," Jane said, "we can't be responsible for another person's death. I can't anyway."

Ramsay nodded. "We'll be discreet."

The phone rang and Jane snatched it up. "Eleven o'clock at Madame Manon's studio on Bury Road." She signaled Ramsay to write it down, which he'd already done. "We'll be there, Wendy. Be sure your driver stays with the car. I don't want any unpleasantness until we have convinced you I was not part of this."

"I never thought you were," Wendy said, "but Tosh jumps to conclusions."

Jane hung up the handset and then phoned Pauline at work, explaining the arrangements. "Can you be there?"

"I can but we must have Ramsay there too. Is he with you?"

"He's here. We'll meet you at the rear of the salon at eleven, all right?"

Jane finished the phone call and turned to Ramsay saying, "Now, I have to get Mimi ready for her grand entrance."

"There's more?" Ramsay cried. "You've washed and dried her to death, filed and painted her claws. What more should she endure?" He was horrified at the indignities being practiced on the poor dog that was sheltering under his arm.

"She only needs a pink bow on her head, her coat trimmed in spots, and her grubby collar refreshed, and she'll be as she was when she was stolen."

Ramsay shook his head but as none of this sounded too

awful, he let Jane pick up Mimi and carry her off to the window where there was more light. He took Bracken out for a walk, in case Bracken was tempted to offer himself for beautification.

When Ramsay returned at ten-thirty, Mimi did indeed look like the photo he had of her, and she wasn't complaining about her treatment so Ramsay felt fine helping Jane put her in a box before they left the house to drive to the salon.

They were early, but that suited Ramsay. With Bracken, he reconnoitered the streets around the salon to ensure they weren't walking into a trap. He saw Pauline's car park farther down the road, well away from the salon. He smiled. She too wanted to be sure no one could track them back to their places of refuge.

As Pauline arrived beside him, greeting him solemnly with a worried countenance, Ramsay saw over Pauline's shoulder the Daimler appear at the farther end of the street.

"Don't look," he said, "but I think this is Wendy arriving."

The Daimler drew up at the curb outside the salon and Wendy was escorted out by the driver. "Pick me up in an hour," they heard her tell him. The driver watched her go into the shop and returned to the car.

Continuing their conversation, Ramsay and Pauline waited until the car drew away and disappeared down the street.

"Phew," Ramsay said. "So far, so good."

"We need to wait in case he comes back," Pauline replied.

"Then you go on and meet Jane. I'll watch."

Ramsay and Bracken strolled casually along the street, watching every place a man could emerge from if he were returning to the salon and hoping not to be noticed. When Ramsay approached the salon, he saw Pauline signaling him from the back street to join them. With one last sweep of the street, he strode quickly to where the three women were gathered.

"This is Chief Inspector Ramsay," Pauline said, introducing him to Wendy. "He did much of the work."

"Retired Chief Inspector," Ramsay said, shaking Wendy's hand, "I was working on another kidnapped pet case, which led me, and us, to finding your pet."

"But who took him, Inspector?"

"I'm not at liberty to say because the case will be taken over by the authorities," Ramsay said.

"It had to be someone who knew Mimi was with Jane," Wendy said, her eyes examining all three faces looking for confirmation.

"Possibly," Pauline said, "and I'm sure the police will want to ask you who you told or who might have heard you telling someone. We can't be sure how that knowledge got out."

"I can," Wendy said coldly.

To Pauline, Wendy's expression suggested she'd suddenly remembered a moment in time and who was present.

"It's best you let the police deal with these things," Ramsay said.

Wendy nodded. "Would you three like another puzzle to solve? I'll pay whatever it takes."

Pauline didn't like the sound of this. Something in Wendy's voice told her to refuse.

Jane said, "Yes. What is it?"

"Jane," Pauline began but was stopped by Jane waving a hand.

"If you don't want to, go," Jane said. "I've never enjoyed myself so much in years as I have these past days."

Pauline nodded. "I must return to work anyway. We can talk about it later." She left them in earnest conversation and returned to her car.

33

PREVENTING A MURDER

With Pauline and her disapproval gone, Wendy began, "I have a problem, worse even than the loss of Mimi." Hearing her name, Mimi stretched up and licked Wendy's cheek. Wendy snuggled her face to Mimi's, leaving the two sleuths wondering what could possibly be worse than the loss of Mimi in Wendy's life.

Recovering, Wendy said "Whatever happens, you must tell no one what I'm about to tell you. Promise?"

Feeling she was back in junior school, Jane nodded and promised. Ramsay also let it be known he wasn't in the habit of sharing confidential information with others.

"Tosh bought me a tiara for our anniversary," Wendy began. "I wore it the night of our anniversary and then locked it in the safe where I keep all my jewelry." She stopped.

"And?" Jane said. She was concerned at the possibility of Wendy's driver returning and catching them all in conference. He might report what he'd seen to Tosh who would put the worst possible construction on this meeting.

"It was taken from my safe a few days later, along with other pieces," Wendy said quickly.

"Where is the safe?" Ramsay asked, though he was sure he knew.

"In my bedroom," Wendy said. "If I tell Tosh he'll know I've had others in my bedroom and might assume it was a man."

"He wouldn't like that," Jane agreed.

"And was it a man?" Ramsay asked.

A pained expression crossed Wendy's face. "It might have been."

"Wendy!" Jane cried. "Are you mad?"

"It's not what you think. It was a party," Wendy said sulkily.

"Without Tosh?"

"He was away, and my driver needed some time off, so I agreed," Wendy said. "I just wanted some time to call my own. You don't know what it's like being me."

"What made you give the driver the day off and hold a party?" Jane said. "The driver might tell Tosh?"

"It's all right. He can't tell," Wendy said unhappily. "It was a spur of the moment thing." She paused, deciding how much to explain. "He came to me around mid-morning saying his mother had fallen, broken her hip and was in hospital. He looked devastated. I told him I wasn't going anywhere so he could go see his mother."

"Tosh wouldn't like that," Jane said.

Wendy nodded. "I was feeling low right then. Mimi was gone and I was alone in the house so when he left, I thought maybe, just for once, I could have some fun. Tosh was down in London and had already phoned to say he'd arrived safely. He does that to keep me tied to the house," she added bitterly.

"And?" Jane asked, when Wendy showed no sign of continuing.

Wendy gave herself a shake and said, "I called some close friends, and they dropped by. I didn't leave the house, so I hadn't really told lies to Tosh or the driver. The driver was back by late afternoon. His mother died and he was grateful to me for letting him be with her. He swore me to secrecy because Tosh would never accept his mother's death as an excuse to leave me alone with Tosh away."

"I didn't know men like him had mothers," Ramsay said acidly.

"You want us to get the tiara back, I suppose," Jane asked.

"Yes, and before next weekend," Wendy said despairingly. "I thought I was a goner but you finding Mimi gives me hope. You might save me."

Ramsay stared at her in horror. "When at the weekend?"

"Saturday night. Tosh is taking me to a show. We have a box and everything. He wants me to be seen in the tiara. It's not just *my* life that's at stake. It's the driver's too. All he did was spend some final hours with his mother and now this."

"You must realize the tiara and your jewels will be with a fence already," Ramsay said. "The thief won't still have them. They're too dangerous to him, or her."

"But you might find the fence," Wendy cried. "I'll buy them back."

"Who was at this party?" Jane asked.

Wendy listed five names, all well-known to Jane, but only one known to Ramsay, Brian Brereton. This explained his flight from Manchester when the investigations into Mimi's disappearance came round to him. Investigations that might have turned up another theft altogether.

"Brereton," Ramsay said. "Did you see him go into the bedroom during the party?"

Wendy's face was a picture of mixed emotions. "He might have done."

"Wendy," Jane cried. "There's no time for games here. No matter how embarrassing this is for you, it's nothing to what will happen if you aren't wearing that tiara on Saturday night."

Wendy nodded unhappily. "He stayed after the others left. When I woke, he was gone."

"Didn't you check the safe right away?" Ramsay asked.

Wendy shook her head. "There was no reason to. The safe was locked, only I knew where the key was, and anyway I was too busy tidying the place before Tosh came home. I didn't know anything was missing until the next day."

"Have you spoken to the people who were there?' Jane asked.

"No! I don't want anyone to know my jewels are missing. It would get back to Tosh somehow."

"Not even Brereton?"

"I've been trying to talk to him," Wendy said. "Though what could I say? Give the jewelry back? He'd laugh at me. The only way I could harm him is if I told Tosh and if I do that, I'm a dead woman."

"You want us to lean on him?" Ramsay asked.

"I don't know he took them," Wendy said. "One of the others could have taken them and slipped away when we were partying."

"Only if they knew where you kept the key," Ramsay asked. "I'm thinking of the women here. In your conversations with them did you at any time hint about the safe and the key?"

"I'm not sure," Wendy said, miserably. "The girls and I

have get-togethers where we drink and..." she stopped, remembering Ramsay had been a policeman.

"You think a woman more likely?" Jane asked Ramsay.

"I think Wendy is more likely to have told a woman where the key would be, but that doesn't mean she didn't tell a man."

Wendy pleaded, "Can you help?"

"We can try," Jane said. "But there isn't much time."

"You should make plans for an escape on Friday or Saturday," Ramsay said bluntly. "You might want to warn your driver, too."

Wendy nodded unhappily and left them to finish her appointment at the salon.

"You don't think we can find the jewelry before Saturday?" Jane asked Ramsay, as they walked back to the car, Bracken trotting alongside and pulling at the leash in hopes of investigating lamp and gate posts.

"The pet snatchers were right there in front of our eyes, and it took us over a week," Ramsay said, restraining Bracken, while his gaze constantly swept the streets. "I don't see this being any different."

"It has to be one of the five people Wendy entertained that day," Jane objected. "She must have told them."

Ramsay shook his head. "Not necessarily and anyone she did tell could have told someone else and they could have burgled the place whenever Wendy was out."

"She's never out, though," Jane said. "Believe me. She's little more than a privileged prisoner in that house. It had to have been that afternoon when they were in a stupor or when she fell asleep."

"I'll ask my contact for jewelry fences," Ramsay said, unlocking the car doors and ushering Bracken into the rear seat. "I don't hold out much hope."

When they were in the car and Ramsay was starting the engine, Jane asked, "Would a fence take something as identifiable as a tiara?"

"They take them and break them up into stones and metals right away," Ramsay said, "to prevent them being identified. Unless the item is something more precious as a whole piece. I doubt this tiara is one worn by some famous woman in bygone years so it will be the breaking up process in this case."

"Oh," Jane said. "I thought they'd sell the items as they are."

Ramsay shook his head. "Imagine a woman meeting another woman at an event and having her jewelry identified as stolen property. No, unless they're famous pieces and intended only for display, they're recycled."

"Sounds like the scrap metal business," Jane said with a sad laugh.

"That's exactly what it is," Ramsay said. "Only with precious metals and stones."

"What can I do?"

"You know those two women," Ramsay said. "Start with phoning them. Question them. Find out if they knew where the safe key was kept and if they told anyone."

"It's not going to be easy without giving away the theft, but I'll start the moment I'm back at Pauline's place." She paused, brightened, and said, "Maybe soon, now Mimi's safe, I can go back to my apartment."

34

FINDING A STOLEN TIARA

PAULINE WAS unimpressed when she returned home that evening and Jane filled her in on the plans she and Inspector Ramsay had made.

"The reason I don't take sleazy cases is exactly this," Pauline said. "Horrible people doing horrible things to each other, none of them innocent, all of them guilty."

"Wendy and her driver could be killed," Jane cried.

"And whoever we identify as the thief will be too," Pauline said. "The jewels were bought with money from crime and Wendy knew that when she accepted them. The people who have stolen them are themselves thieves. They may not deserve to die either, but they will if we unmask them."

"I don't understand what made them think robbing a gangster's wife was a good idea," Jane said, shaking her head.

"Their critical faculties were almost certainly overcome by drink and drugs," Pauline said. "A lawyer could get a reduced sentence on that alone, from a regular judge. But they aren't going to be judged by someone like you and me, are they?"

"So, you won't help?"

Pauline bit her lip. Everything she held dear said no. Only, she'd met Wendy, and felt sorry for the poor woman, and she hadn't met the partygoers.

"I'll help but this is the end, Jane. I won't do any more for people like these. If you want to spend your life among them, so be it. I will not."

Jane's expression said she now realized the danger. "I plan to move to London the moment this is over. Wendy might persuade Tosh I wasn't involved this time but if anything happens in the future, this will color his view of me. I won't get a second chance."

"See you keep to that," Pauline said. "Now, you said you've phoned the two women, what did you learn from them?"

"That they told no one about the location of Wendy's safe key," Jane said.

"But they knew where it was kept?"

Jane grinned. "Exactly. Whatever Wendy was taking that day made her indiscreet. It seems she kept it somewhere sexually suggestive and decided to share the joke with the group."

"So," Pauline said, shaking her head in dismay at Wendy's behavior, "if they're telling the truth, it's one of the five of them."

"My money is on Brereton," Jane said. "Opportunity, means, and I'm not exactly going out on a limb here, motive."

"What motive?"

"One of the two women told me he owes lots of money to his drug supplier," Jane said. "I've thought for some time his supplier is the woman's husband and her knowing this confirms it."

"You told me Brereton was loaded with money," Pauline cried. "Now you say he owes money."

"People who *have* money, owe money," Jane said. "He has a nice house, a big car, the latest fashions, and he's always hosting parties. He has money. It's just he owes some too."

Pauline bit her tongue on a sharp response and instead asked, "Does the husband you think Brereton owes money to work for your friend Tosh? You also said Tosh wouldn't have drugs in his house."

"In his house," Jane said, "that's true. Doesn't mean he's against people he doesn't care about taking them. Why would it?"

"Does that woman's husband work for Tosh?" Pauline demanded.

"Yes," Jane snapped back, unhappy at being forced to admit she knew this.

Pauline shook her head. "Jane, this is seriously wrong. I don't believe you can close your eyes to this. People's lives are ruined with drugs."

"They're just uppers and downers," Jane protested. "Not hardline stuff like heroin. Everybody takes them. It's how we party all night."

"I wish you'd told me this earlier," Pauline began.

Jane interjected, "You and your police friend would have been all over us, me included."

"Perhaps," Pauline replied. "It doesn't matter now. We need to get focused on that woman; she could just be distracting us away from herself. It still leaves me suspicious of Brereton, but it moves this woman up to a close second."

"You think we should look further into both?"

"If Brereton is in London, and he has the jewels, it's all over for Wendy," Pauline said. "Only Inspector Ramsay with his contacts could get something on him. We need to focus on the woman who wants us to look Brereton's way."

"Phone the inspector now," Jane said. "Get him started because Brereton is the most likely one. He was the one who stayed behind and was gone before Wendy woke up."

Inspector Ramsay's answer was deflating. He'd already spoken to an old colleague in the London force after the long nighttime chase and Brereton was nowhere to be found.

"London's a big place," Pauline said to Jane who was sure the London police were doing nothing. "It takes time."

"And he's probably in a rented place, not working, and has no known associates down there," Ramsay said. "He's just laying low."

"That might be a good thing," Pauline said. "It may mean he hasn't yet risked selling the jewels to a fence."

"It may," Ramsay said, though his voice suggested he thought it unlikely.

"They must find him," Jane cried.

"You can help, Jane," Ramsay said. "Question his friends and colleagues about where he might be in London. Someone might know."

"I'll phone around the moment we're finished," Jane said.

"Did you have any success with jewelry fences, Inspector?" Pauline asked.

"I have a list and I visited the most likely two this afternoon," Ramsay replied. "It would help if I had a photo of the missing items. Wendy's descriptions aren't sparking any recognition among the people I've talked to so far."

Jane laughed. "Do those people ever tell the police anything?"

"They are cagey about their replies, as a rule," Ramsay said. "Today I got the feeling their denials were genuine. Still, your point is correct. I don't take their word on very much."

"Your experience, Inspector, must mean you're generally right about them," Pauline said.

"It gives me an advantage," Ramsay agreed. "I've listened to those kinds of people all my working life and can generally spot when there's something not right. Today, I didn't get that."

"How many are on the list?" Jane asked.

"Four. I'll do the other two tomorrow morning. By lunchtime I should have an idea about where the tiara is or a reasonable assumption that it isn't yet being offered for sale."

"If it's Brereton," Jane said, "and if he needs money quickly, it's the London buyers we need to talk to."

"There are many more fences in London than Manchester," Ramsay said, "but we don't really know for sure he's in London. I didn't follow him there. He may have friends somewhere near, but not in, London. Oxford, maybe."

"We can't have the police in every town and village between Birmingham and London looking for him," Pauline said. "Jane, you must see what you can do."

Jane was too deep in thought to notice she was being spoken to, until Pauline said, "Jane!"

"What?"

"Find us a contact for Brereton from among his friends."

"I'm going to, but I've just thought of something."

"And what's that?"

"We have six suspects because we only have Wendy's word the tiara was in the safe and is now gone," Jane said.

"Surely she wouldn't put her life at risk with an investigation if it isn't missing," Ramsay said.

"How do we know she is?" Jane said stubbornly. "Maybe there is no show on Saturday and she's setting up one of those so-called friends for Tosh to eliminate."

"Then we need to include Tosh himself," Ramsay said. "Perhaps he came back early that day, found Wendy asleep, the house in a mess, evidence she hadn't gone to bed alone, and decided to give her the scare of her life, or worse?"

"Seven then," Pauline said, shaking her head. "We can't solve this before Saturday – if we even need to."

The three fell into thoughtful silence while they mulled over these additional possibilities.

"I think," Ramsay suggested, "we stick with our plan. If it's Wendy or Tosh, we have no way of intervening so we should follow the leads we're working on."

Pauline and Jane exchanged glances before Pauline shrugged and said, "It's possible we'll stumble on something that points to Tosh and Wendy while we investigate the others."

"Anything's possible," Ramsay said wryly.

"We should talk again at lunchtime tomorrow," Jane said. "I'll have enough people questioned to have an idea if there's a hope of finding Brereton, and you, Inspector, should have talked to all the local fences."

There was agreement on this, and the call ended. Jane immediately began searching for Brereton information among their circle of friends and acquaintances.

35

BRERETON FOUND BUT NO TIARA

LUNCHTIME THE FOLLOWING DAY, Pauline had driven back to her apartment and was ready to talk when Ramsay called.

"Have you anything to report, Inspector?" she asked.

"No, though I think one of the fences I spoke to today wasn't entirely honest in his answers," Ramsay said. "I've asked Logan for more on the man. What about Jane and Brereton's friends?"

"Nobody claims to know anywhere down London way where he might be found," Jane said. "I still have more to phone, though."

"Let's talk again this evening," Pauline said. "We need a breakthrough soon if we're to find that tiara in time for Wendy to wear it on Saturday."

The phone call that evening provided some hope. Jane had discovered Brereton did have a sister who lived in a small village north of London.

"Then tomorrow we find her," Ramsay said. "Will you come with us, Miss Riddell?"

"I have meetings I can't miss tomorrow," Pauline said. The storm created by her report was still raging among the company's executives. Pauline would have been happy to take the day off to escape the furor, only her conscience wouldn't let her.

"Then it's just us, Inspector," Jane said.

"We must start early," Ramsay said. "Six am at the latest."

Jane mumbled her agreement. Ramsay demanded a fully committed agreement and Jane eventually confirmed she'd be ready then.

Pauline was still chuckling when she asked, "Did you have any success with that shifty fence, Inspector?"

"Yes and no. Long story short, he was hiding something but not what we're looking for."

"Then tomorrow is where we bring this to a conclusion," Jane said. "This investigating isn't as difficult as I'd been led to believe."

* * *

BRERETON'S CAR standing in the driveway of a small, modern, semi-detached bungalow made finding the house easy. His sister lived almost at the entrance to a new housing development that looked grafted onto an old rural village.

Ramsay parked behind the Westminster to prevent it leaving should Brereton make a run for it, and they knocked on the house door. It was opened by a young woman with a child on her hip.

"Is Brian here?" Jane asked. "It's Jane Riddell."

The woman called inside, "Brian. It's for you. Jane Riddell?"

Brereton appeared in the hall behind his sister and frowned at Jane. "What are you doing here?"

"Looking for you," Jane replied. She paused and then added, "And Wendy's tiara."

Brereton's face was a picture of incomprehension. "I haven't got Wendy's, or anyone's, tiara. Why would I?"

"Then where is it?" Jane asked.

He shook his head. "How should I know? I didn't even know it was missing."

"Then why are you here and not in your house?" Jane asked.

"Somebody was trying to frame me for Wendy's dog going missing." His gaze moved to Ramsay and recognition sparked in his eyes. "Him, to be exact."

"Wendy says you were the only one alone in the room from where it was taken," Jane continued.

"At that impromptu party she held, she told us all where the key was," Brereton said. "Any of them could have come back and taken the tiara when Wendy and I were asleep."

"You were asleep?" Ramsay asked. "You're in bed with a dangerous gangster's wife and you fell asleep? You can't expect us to believe that."

"We'd had a lot to drink," Brereton said sheepishly. "Lunacy, I know. The moment I realized where I was and what had happened, I got out of there. I didn't go looking for more trouble by stealing tiaras."

Ramsay considered this. It made sense, but if it wasn't Brereton, who was it?

"Inspector Ramsay is right, Brian," Jane said. "No matter how drunk you were, you wouldn't be mad enough to fall asleep there."

"It wasn't just drink," Brereton muttered. "And you can believe me or not, that's what happened. I'm having nightmares about it." He shuddered.

"Do you think Wendy would've even mentioned this to us if she didn't believe you took it?" Ramsay asked.

"Come inside," Brereton's sister said. "We can't stay like this. Everyone on the street will start noticing." She stepped back from the doorway and motioned them to enter with a nod of her head.

"I wouldn't put anything past her," Brereton said, as he led them into the lounge and gestured for them to sit on a couch, while he took an armchair opposite.

"Then you'll have no objection to us looking through your car and your room," Ramsay said. He had no authority to ask, but he hoped Brereton wouldn't object if he were innocent.

Brereton frowned. "You can," he said, "but I'm not having a woman going through my things."

Jane was about to point out they'd spent intimate time together but caught Ramsay's glance.

"Worried I'll see your dirty magazines, Brian?" She laughed. Brereton didn't.

"Let's start with the car," Ramsay interjected, determined not to lose the opportunity he'd been given.

Ramsay and Brereton left the room and Jane could see, through the room's large window, Ramsay diligently searching Brereton's car.

"You haven't seen a tiara or other pieces of jewelry, have you?" Jane asked Brereton's sister.

She shook her head. "No and I think I would, unless it's in the car. I've been in and out of his room these past days and there's nowhere to hide anything. We're still new in the house. The room Brian is in has no more than a bed and a dresser."

"The thing is, the woman who claims she lost it, says her life may be in danger if she doesn't have it to wear when she goes out with her husband on Saturday. She looked genuinely terrified when she told us this."

"The one good thing I hope will come from what's happened is he won't be able to go back there no matter what the outcome," Brereton's sister replied. "I've pleaded with him to leave those people, but he's always been one for the bright lights."

Jane nodded ruefully. "That's me too, I'm afraid. My sister says it's madness to be part of this crowd and I've always told her she doesn't understand. These past days, I've come to see bad things could happen not just to others but to me as well."

"Tell Brian that before you go. He won't listen to me."

Ramsay and Brereton reentered the house and headed up the stairs off the hall.

"It wasn't in the car, then," Jane said sadly. "We hoped Brian would have it and he'd realize the best thing for everyone would be for us to return it to Wendy before her husband even suspected it was missing."

"And now?"

"And now we're in the soup," Jane said. "If the tiara is missing, and Wendy was very convincing, then we have a handful of suspects and no time to investigate them all."

Ramsay and Brereton returned to the lounge and Ramsay shook his head at Jane's quizzical expression.

"Brian," his sister said, "please. If you have these things give them to Jane and she'll return them to Wendy. That way no one gets hurt."

"I swear to you. I woke that afternoon and when I realized where I was, I ran. Tiaras never entered my head. I owe money, it's true, but stealing from Tosh and Wendy would be a death sentence, whether it was a dog or jewelry. I'm not that stupid."

"There were four others at the party," Jane said. "Would any of them take that chance? Particularly if they thought you'd get the blame?"

Brereton shook his head. "I don't think so. We all know what Tosh is like."

"Might any of them want to see you harmed?" Ramsay asked.

"Everyone has small grievances against their friends," Brereton said, "but this is way beyond that. No, I don't believe it."

"There's nothing you can think of that might help us?" Ramsay asked. "Anything, at all?"

Brereton shook his head. "Nothing. I didn't even know about these missing jewels until now. Now I do, I know I must disappear for good."

"You imagined you could go back?" Jane cried, astounded at such optimism.

Brereton flushed red. "I thought the dog would show up, there'd be no connection to me, and I could return to pick up where we'd all left off. Now, I know I can't."

Jane nodded. "To be honest, I thought the same thing at first, but neither of us can go back. Tosh will think there's no smoke without fire."

"Well, we must be making our way back to Manchester," Ramsay said to Jane, "and begin looking into those other four." He rose, thanked Brereton's sister for letting them talk privately, and he and Jane left the house.

"What do we do now?" Jane asked, as Ramsay was backing the car out of the drive.

"Whatever it is, it has to be fast," he replied, as they began their long drive back.

36

MISS RIDDELL STEPS IN

AFTER RAMSAY AND JANE LEFT, Pauline drove to work deep in thought. By mid-morning, when everyone in the offices around her was buying or eating their morning snack and the tea trolley, with its too talkative tea lady, had left her office, Pauline took the chance and phoned.

"Wendy," Pauline said, when she heard the phone picked up. "It's Pauline Riddell. Do you remember? I'm Jane's sister. I'm glad I could catch you in."

"I remember," Wendy replied shortly. "What is it you want?"

"I want you to tell the truth," Pauline said.

"About what?"

"About that afternoon you spent with Mr. Brereton and what happened to your jewels."

"You're calling me a liar?"

"I'm saying you're rightly frightened of your husband finding out you were alone with Brian Brereton. I would be too, in your position, and you know Jane well enough to invent this frightening story to get her to find Brereton."

"Who told you this rubbish?"

"Nobody told me," Pauline said. "It's the only thing that makes sense. None of your friends would rob your safe. You know it and I know it."

"What of it," Wendy said. "I need him found."

"And you knew Jane would help if she thought your life in danger."

"If you know all this, what are we talking about here?'

"We're talking about saving lives, Wendy," Pauline responded. "Brereton's and possibly yours and your driver's. I assume he'd do the actual killing?"

Wendy laughed. "He has no choice. He's as scared as I am."

"Look, you want the evidence of what happened that day gone for good. I understand that, and Mr. Brereton will too when it's put to him in the right way."

"The right way is for him to disappear off the face of the earth," Wendy said, bluntly.

"I'm sure he could be persuaded to emigrate and that would be just as good."

"He would always be there," Wendy said.

"Stand your driver down, Wendy," Pauline said. "Murder will only make things worse."

"Look, I'll mind my business and you mind yours – or I might begin to think you're a threat too."

"I'm not and Mr. Brereton needn't be either. I'm sure he's as frightened as you are about Tosh learning what happened. He'll stay silent, you can be sure."

"You're right, the tiara isn't gone, but I want to be sure he stays silent." Wendy chuckled. "The same way Lance Delaval is staying silent."

"Delaval's dead?"

"An overdose," Wendy said. "It was always going to happen; he's been getting more and more hooked and more and more erratic this past year. Mimi was the last straw."

"Why do you think it was him who stole Mimi?" Pauline asked, hoping not to hear Jane had told her.

"I remembered he knew where Mimi was and how desperate he'd become," Wendy said. "Even I can make that sum add up."

Pauline's blood froze. The casual violence these people took for granted was beyond her. "That wouldn't be enough in a court of law," she began. Wendy's laughter stopped her.

When Wendy stopped laughing, Pauline said, "We'll find Brereton and send him overseas. There's no need for more ugliness."

"Good luck with that," Wendy said.

"His own terror should be enough. What has he done to warrant this?"

"Nothing," Wendy said. "He did nothing – and put my life at risk doing it." The phone slammed down, making Pauline jump with the shock.

She slowly placed the handset on its rest. When Wendy said Brereton would stay silent, did she mean her driver was already on the way to Brereton's sister's house? After all, if Jane had found Brereton by asking around, Wendy and her driver could as well. Could Pauline persuade the police to get to Brereton's sister's house before Wendy's driver found it? Or did the driver follow Ramsay's car today? Wild thoughts were still bouncing around inside her head when her boss knocked on the door and entered. "Pauline, we're wanted," he said, "and not in a good way."

She picked up the folder of notes she kept permanently ready to hand and followed him to the next meeting.

. . .

Pauline was already back at her apartment when Jane and Ramsay returned. She listened without interruption as they recounted their interview with Brereton.

"So, you see," Ramsay said, "we're back to square one."

"Not exactly," Pauline said. She waited until their puzzlement had fully registered. "You see, the tiara was never stolen. Wendy used its 'theft' so we would find Brereton for her."

"Why?" Jane cried.

"When she woke that day, the drink and excitement had worn off and she realized what she'd done. She knew immediately she would never be safe with Brereton alive."

"We must warn him," Ramsay said.

"Do you have a phone number?" Pauline asked.

"They don't have a phone," Jane said. "She wouldn't kill him, would she?"

"I expect she already has," Pauline said. "Lance Delaval is dead."

"We didn't set her on him as well, did we?" Jane cried.

"I fear we did," Ramsay said, "when we asked her to think again who knew where Mimi was."

"Can we find a way to bring her to justice?" Jane asked.

"We can tell the police what we know," Ramsay said.

"We should do that," Jane said.

Pauline shook her head. "You should both leave and never return here. We have no evidence to support what we know, and our informing will make us known to whichever officers are in Tosh's pocket."

Ramsay shook his head. "That's not the advice I would expect from Miss Riddell."

"Nevertheless, it's the advice I'm giving, Inspector," Pauline replied. "Where I work there's a lot of materials coming in, and products going out, through the docks, so I asked our shipping people about Tosh and Corrigan and that was their advice. I'm passing it on to you."

"We must do something. Running away isn't right," Jane said.

"I'm afraid I agree with your sister again, Jane, but it bothers me to leave Brereton out there as a walking dead man," Ramsay said.

"Write a short letter now and get it in the post. He may get it by the morning mail delivery if you can find a mailbox not yet emptied. He'll get it by the second post tomorrow, for sure."

Ramsay shook his head. "I'm driving down there right now. Either of you coming?"

Pauline frowned. "I must be in work tomorrow. Things are not going well there either."

"I'll go with you, Inspector," Jane said. "Let me put on warmer clothes for the nighttime and we'll leave." She hurried off into the bathroom with her leather jumpsuit while Ramsay phoned the B&B to warn his landlady he wouldn't be home, and to ask her to look after Bracken again tomorrow.

"Mr. Ramsay," she began in a chilly tone.

"You're quite right," Ramsay interjected, "add pet minding to my bill."

With Jane changed, and a flask of tea for the journey, they bade Pauline goodnight and began the long, slow drive back down south.

"Do you think Pauline's right?" Jane asked, as she and Ramsay joined the major road to the south.

"She usually is, and this time will likely be no exception."

"Then why go if he's already dead?"

"Because he might not be," Ramsay said. "Wendy's driver will wait until Brereton is alone and that may not have happened yet."

"So, if we get to the house before Brian leaves it, we might yet save him?"

"It's possible," Ramsay replied. "It's worth a try."

"But Brian can't stay indoors forever," Jane said, considering the options.

"If he has a passport, we can escort him to Heathrow and put him on a plane to Paris or somewhere far from here. After that, it's up to him."

"He once mentioned a cousin in Canada," Jane said.

"That will do as a start. First, we must get to him before that driver does."

The hours rolled by in silence as they made their way south. Every stop for fuel was agony for Jane as it increased the time when Brian may step outside and become a target. Once midnight was passed, they both relaxed. It seemed unlikely Brian or anyone would go outside that late in a small village with no night life.

THE VILLAGE WAS in darkness when they pulled off the main road and parked outside Brereton's sister's house.

"It looks like nothing has happened here," Ramsay said, sighing with relief, "otherwise there'd be signs of a crime scene or other upheaval."

Jane nodded. "Do we knock or wait until morning?"

"We ring the bell," Ramsay replied. "I'm not sitting here until they wake."

"It's best," Jane said. "Brian should know what he's up against as soon as possible. For all we know, Wendy's driver is climbing in a window at the back of the house right now."

Ramsay laughed. "I think it will be made to look more like an accident rather than him being murdered in his bed. Anyway, I don't think the driver, or Wendy, would want Brereton's sister and family hurt in any way."

They opened the car doors and stepped outside. The air was cold after the warmth of the car, making Jane shiver.

The garden gate squealed on its hinges as they passed through. It sounded loud enough to wake the household, but no lights came on. Brereton's car was still on the drive and Ramsay quickly looked inside. No one was in the car, and nothing seemed out of place.

"He wouldn't be hiding in there," Jane said, giggling.

Ramsay grinned. "You never know what can be anywhere," he said, as they made their way to the door and rang the bell.

A light came on upstairs and then downstairs. The door opened and a young man in a dressing gown stared at them in surprise.

"I thought you were…" he began, then stopped. "Who are you and what do you want?"

Ramsay explained they'd been here only hours before and had returned to warn Mr. Brereton he might be in danger.

The man frowned, puzzled. "In danger?"

"Yes," Jane said. "We've since learned someone wants him removed."

"He was hit by a car this evening," the man said. "My missus is at the hospital now."

"Badly hurt?" Ramsay asked.

"Bad enough, but they say he'll live."

"Did they get the driver?" Jane asked.

The man shook his head. "The swine didn't even stop to see if Brian was all right."

"Did anyone recognize the car?"

"Police say they were told it was a big car, a Jaguar or Humber, something of that kind. It was dark, you see. Brian was walking back from the pub." He was about to go on when a wailing from inside the house made him turn. "Mary's awake," he said. "I have to go."

"Before you go, which hospital?" Ramsay asked.

The man gave the name and directions before closing the door.

"We need to speak to Brereton or his sister," Ramsay said. "He needs to be on a boat or a plane the moment he can walk."

They encountered resistance from the night staff who weren't willing to have visitors wandering the wards in the wee small hours of the night. In the end, Brereton's sister came out to them. They explained their errand and told her what she must tell her brother before he was released from the hospital.

"I knew he was in with a bad crowd," Brereton's sister said. "I just didn't know it was this bad."

Jane felt her cheeks flushing. "You must make him leave."

The woman nodded. "I'll tell him. Whether he'll do as you say, I can't promise."

"You must make him," Ramsay said. "He survived this attack but if he stays in this country, they'll come for him again. Two people terrified for their own lives won't let him live."

She nodded. "I'll do all I can. If necessary, we'll drive him to Heathrow Airport and put him on a plane."

Jane and Ramsay made their way back to Ramsay's car. With the excitement gone, they felt drained, exhausted.

"It's getting light," Jane said. "We should find a worker's café open. Strong coffee and breakfast might just get us back to Manchester before we fall asleep."

"There were roadside food vans at that truck stop we passed on our way into the village," Ramsay replied. "I don't think they'll be open yet, but we could nap there until they are."

He was right. They parked and slept until the noise of people talking, and the smell of bacon frying, woke them.

"Simple food is always the best," Jane said, munching on a bacon sandwich.

Ramsay nodded. "Everything tastes good when you're hungry." After his long fast and the wretched night, his own bun with fried bacon and egg tasted like heaven.

"Should we phone Pauline and tell her that while we were too late to stop Brereton being attacked, our warning might still save his life?" Jane asked as they made their way back to the car.

"Yes," Ramsay replied. "The car needs fuel. You can phone at the next service station while I fill up. She'll be glad to hear of our 'sort of' success." He slammed the door and turned the ignition key.

"I can't see why." Jane said. "I just think she should know." She lifted her coat from the back seat and wrapped it over herself, tucking it in at each side of the seat.

Ramsay sighed. "Because, if Brereton was dead, your sister would have to inform the police about everything she knows. Now we know he isn't, and he's been warned, whatever happens to him after this is his concern, not ours."

Jane nodded. "You're right. And for once I agree with Pauline. If Brian leaves the country and if we all just 'fade away' as the Rolling Stones so recently sang, Wendy will forget any of this happened."

"Rolling who?" Ramsay asked.

Jane sighed, shook her head, and closed her eyes. It would have been nice to have borrowed Brian's car for the drive back; it had a radio. Ramsay's old Ford didn't.

37

PARTING OF THE WAYS

Two days later, the three sleuths were back in Pauline's apartment. The days of rest had lifted their spirits but not their underlying anxiety for the future. Pauline and Ramsay sipped cups of tea while Jane, who'd refused tea, was working her way through a large vodka and tonic.

She was the first to speak about the recent events. "I'm disappointed there was no great crime lord hiding behind the pet snatches," she said wistfully. "That would have been a great start to my career."

"What career?" Pauline asked sharply. The last thing she wanted to hear was that her sister was setting out to be a detective. A more rackety investigator would be hard to find anywhere. She would soon end up in a concrete bridge foundation.

"Oh, I'm still going to do pet grooming for the stars," Jane explained, "but I plan to take on discreet commissions solving mysteries. Celebrities always have grievances and there are plenty of petty feuds I could solve. I think I'll be booked out when it becomes known I'm a super-sleuth who does pet grooming as a cover."

"Jane," Pauline said slowly, "this time it was only one nasty man who wanted money for his drug habit and another who thought the world owed him more than it was giving. Neither of them was a dangerous crime lord, to use your words. But next time it *might* be a gangland boss who doesn't care who gets killed so long as his name doesn't make it out into the open. Don't do it."

"Pooh," Jane said airily. "For someone who's famous for sleuthing, you are the most chicken-hearted character I know."

Pauline reddened but kept her temper. "Sensible people take sensible risks, Jane. Not wild gestures that will get them killed for nothing useful."

"You needn't worry," Jane said scornfully. "You won't be called in again to rescue me. I'm going to London."

"What? When?"

"Right away," Jane said. "One of my best clients, and a good friend, is already down there and wants me to look after their dogs. She says no one else will do. I understand her pets, you see."

"What about your salon here?"

"I'll sell it and open or buy one there. A smart one on Carnaby Street or the Kings Road," Jane said. "With Cyn as my introduction to London's swinging scene, I'll be set up in no time."

"I hope you'll use a new name," Pauline said. "Until Tosh and Wendy have forgotten you, you're still at risk."

"Pfft, it's already forgotten," Jane said.

Pauline shook her head. In truth, she thought putting some distance between Jane and Tosh would be a good thing. After hearing of Jane's part in rescuing Mimi in a way that left him unscathed, the wily old gangster had given the impression he'd forgiven her, but Pauline suspected sometime, somewhere, Jane would suffer for what had happened.

"What does Cyn do?" Pauline asked.

"I told you about her," Jane cried. "Don't you ever listen? She's the girlfriend of *The Shades of Blue's* bassist and song writer and she knows everyone."

Guessing at the lifestyle of these people, Pauline could well believe Cyn 'knew' them all. It horrified her to think Jane could look at that world and want to be part of it. None of the Riddell children had been brought up this way and none but Jane would envy those who took part. Still, she couldn't help feeling it was for the best that Jane was far enough away not to want to be a sleuthing team.

"If you're leaving, Jane, would you tell me the name of your drug dealing friend?" Pauline asked. "The one who Delaval owed money to?"

"No, I won't," Jane said. "If the police start sniffing around the moment I leave, Tosh will know exactly who to blame."

"Jane's right," Ramsay said. "It would be satisfying to add that man Tosh and his gang to our score card but not safe for Jane."

Pauline nodded ruefully in agreement. "But I can't forgive Wendy for having Lance Delaval killed."

"But we don't know she did," Ramsay said. "She may only have taken credit for his death to impress you with her toughness. A queen likes to have respect too."

Pauline nodded. "Possibly. And you, Inspector? What have you planned now we're free of this dog's breakfast of a case?"

He laughed and stroked Bracken's head. "Dog's breakfast is right, but Bracken wouldn't thank you for this mess we helped clean up. I'm going to continue rambling around the country and hope no one asks my advice about some local mystery when I arrive anywhere."

"You'll miss it," Pauline replied. "You know you will."

"I expect I shall," he said, scratching under his dog's chin. "Still, Bracken will keep my feet on the ground and stop me taking on any more sleuthing cases. This began as what I first thought was a silly puzzle, but before I knew it, it became a serious crime, then two crimes. I let those crimes slide thinking it was for the best. After all, the pets were found and restored to their owners, and no one was hurt over it. I thought it was over, but it wasn't, and lives were suddenly in danger. What happened to Brereton was enough of a warning for me. I've already had one near miss and it cost me my job. *If* I ever get involved again, I'll follow the 'Miss Riddell Rule' – no sordid crime."

Pauline smiled. "And I was fortunate this time. Hardly anyone knew I was even in it, but it reminded me once again to follow my own advice. My world is one of respectable people who, through force of circumstances, do something wrong but haven't the courage to face up to what they've done."

"All in all, though," Ramsay said, "we made a good team, don't you think? A somewhat quirky mystery team, I'll grant you, but we all contributed one way or another, especially Bracken." He patted Bracken who grinned, happy to have the attention.

"We were a good team for our one and only case together," Pauline agreed.

"Then here's to our separate futures," Jane said, raising her glass.

"Our separate futures," Pauline and Ramsay agreed, toasting with their teacups.

. . .

THANK you for reading my book. If you love this book, Miss Riddell and the Pet Thefts, please, *please,* don't forget to leave a review! Every review matters and it matters a lot!

CLICK HERE to read the next book in the Miss Riddell series:

Miss Riddell and the Heiress

AND TO KEEP up-to-date with all things Miss Riddell, there's also my monthly Newsletter: https://landing.mailerlite.com/webforms/landing/x7a9e4

BONUS CONTENT

An excerpt from Sassy Senior Sleuths on the Trail

Halloween Murder in New Orleans -- 2003

Chapter 1: Day One, October 28

"The outskirts of New Orleans had me worried," Pauline said to her companion, Nona, as their taxi dropped them off at their hotel in the French Quarter. "Flying in and seeing all those industrial plants had me thinking we'd misunderstood the city. The tourist office doesn't mention what a huge place this is now."

"It is quite a contrast to the French Quarter," Nona agreed. "Still, this old part of the city looks like its romantic image and we're here now."

Pauline nodded, looking with satisfaction at the square in front of the hotel with its still flowering shrubs. "It certainly does. And they're all dressed for Halloween too." She pointed at decorations that were hanging from lamps and trees.

"Those old streetlamps will look wonderful when darkness falls," Nona agreed, before making her way into the hotel lobby.

"Welcome, ladies," the receptionist said. "Are you with the Haunted New Orleans Halloween Tour?"

Nona confirmed they were and gave her their names.

As the receptionist collected their keys and entered their arrival details, she continued, "Your tour guide will be here at 4 pm to meet you all and confirm the itinerary. You'll be meeting in the Lafitte Room, which is here on the ground floor."

"We'll be there," Pauline said, as she took her room key from the receptionist.

The receptionist smiled. "Don't be late. I hear there are free drinks to welcome you all."

Nona and Pauline weren't late, but the room was already packed when they arrived. The receptionist had clearly told everyone to be early. Around twenty people were being offered luridly orange and black drinks by two servers in what looked like Addams Family costumes.

Pauline was thankful that the tray of drinks being offered to the two senior sleuths also had on it sparkling wine and not just the brightly colored cocktails. She took a glass, while Nona took an orange concoction with a blood-red umbrella poking from it.

"What is it?" Pauline asked, when Nona had taken a sip.

"No idea but it tastes like pumpkin pie so it can't be bad," Nona replied, grinning.

Pauline sipped her sparkling wine and surveyed the rest of the tour party. "I thought it would be an older crowd," she said.

Nona nodded. "I did too but it seems everyone likes Halloween and haunted cities."

The group was, as they'd seen, mixed. Some younger people, already wearing costumes though October 31st was three days away, some middle-aged, a little more serious but still flighty looking to Pauline's way of thinking, and the rest, like the sleuths, retired people here to see the city as much as the festivities.

"I like that witch," Nona said, pointing at a young woman in a black cape and pointed hat.

"It's very well done," Pauline agreed. The young woman's hair was as blue-black as a raven's wing, her eyes were surrounded by makeup that made them stand out from her pale face. Her lips too were prominent, a thin red slit that looked more like a wound than a mouth.

"What about the young man," Nona said, "the werewolf."

Pauline followed Nona's gaze to the farther corner of the room where a slim werewolf was sipping at one of the black cocktails. "I don't think he's confident enough to be a werewolf."

"Here's our leader," Nona said, gesturing toward a smiling woman who had stepped onto the dais at the end of the room.

After the crowd quieted down, the tour leader began, "Welcome, everyone, to this year's New Orleans Halloween Extravaganza. My name is Jolene and I have the pleasure of being your host and guide for the next five days. You may come to me with any concerns or questions you have."

The woman continued but Pauline's mind returned to studying their tour companions. The young werewolf had moved to where he could hear and see but he still looked nervous and awkward.

A middle-aged couple were also in Halloween costumes, Dracula and his victim, Pauline guessed. They were in good spirits, much more so than one glass of blood-red cocktail would have inspired. Celebrating an anniversary, perhaps, Pauline mused.

A young man stood apart from the crowd scowling; he was evidently not impressed. He's going to be a bore, Pauline decided. He's going to 'debunk' everything the guide and anyone else tells us or who dares to suggest the supernatural is real. His grim expression was enough to unnerve the tour guide, Pauline thought, but she studiously avoided his eye.

Nona nudged Pauline and whispered, "do you see how the werewolf watches the witch?"

Pauline followed Nona's gaze. "You're right. He's fixated on her. I doubt he's heard a word Jolene has said." She looked at the other members of the group and was surprised to see the grimly scowling young man also staring at the witch.

"There's another one," she whispered to Nona, pointing discreetly.

Nona nodded. "My psychic powers tell me there's a strong chance of violence in our near futures," she said, chuckling.

"They must have known each other from before," Pauline said. "That depth of lovesickness doesn't happen right away."

"I checked the register," Nona said. "Most of the people on the tour are from Hopeburg, West Virginia, so I think a travel agency from there must have advertised heavily."

"That would explain it," Pauline agreed, nodding. "My guess is when those two young men heard their beloved had signed up to the tour, they did too. I thought it was odd that two single young men would be on a tour like this."

Nona, however, was distracted and hardly seemed to notice Pauline was speaking. "What is it?" Pauline asked, trying to follow Nona's gaze to see what was so interesting.

"It isn't just the two young men," Nona whispered, "look at the goofy couple."

Pauline looked. The man was watching the witch with an adoring gaze that set off alarm bells in Pauline's head. A quick glance at the wife confirmed her fears. If looks could kill, that husband would already be dead on the floor.

"I'm glad this is only four days," Pauline said. "Otherwise, we might have a murder on our hands."

Nona laughed. "How else would we know we're on vacation?"

Jolene finished speaking and invited everyone to enjoy the drinks and introduce themselves. She would be available for questions at a desk in the corner.

"We should mingle," Pauline said, "especially with the love triangle we think we spotted."

Nona laughed. "We may be reading too much into the glances we saw."

Pauline nodded. "Still, it can't do any harm to see if we were right."

"That's an impressive costume," Nona said, grabbing the witch's arm as she passed by. "You really like to get into the mood, I guess."

The witch smiled broadly. "I do," she said. "I know witches didn't really dress this way, but I can't help it. I love everything about the supernatural, don't you?"

Nona grinned. "I like the party side of it. I'm Nona, by the way. This is my friend, and fellow sleuth, Pauline."

They shook hands, as the witch introduced herself as Chrissie.

"Tell me, Chrissie," Pauline asked, "do you know the werewolf over there?" She pointed to the stage where the young man was now watching them intently.

Chrissie laughed. "That's Simon. He's besotted with me, and I can't stand him." She paused, then added, "I don't mean there's anything wrong with him but he's just a boy, really. Tongue-tied and tortured by first love. I remember those days myself, but it shouldn't be happening to a twenty-two-year-old."

"You seem to know a lot about him," Nona said.

"Oh, yes. We're all from Hopeburg, you see," Chrissie said. "Half our town is here, sadly."

"Then you'll know the grumpy fellow over there." Pauline pointed to the other side of the room.

"Sure do. That's Tom. He's seen the light, born again again as a first-class killjoy," Chrissie replied. "He and I went out together and he pretended he too believed in the supernatural. When I realized he didn't, he began lecturing me and I dumped him."

"Why would he come on this tour, then," Nona asked.

"To save me, I expect, or to stop me hooking up with Simon."

"Then he knows Simon?"

"We work in the same company," Chrissie said. "Actually, the whole town does. There's nowhere else to work."

"The older couple, as well?" Nona asked, pointing to the couple trying not to look their way.

"Mr. Oddfellow is one of the managers," Chrissie said. "His wife is a homebody, so I don't know her."

"Did you know everyone was coming?" Pauline asked. "Or did you only find out when you met on the plane?"

Chrissie laughed. "Almost. I did know, but this trip is something I've had in mind for a while. I've read so much about New Orleans and its supernatural side, I couldn't resist when Grace, my friend, and the local travel agent, told me about it. There was no way I was going to cancel because a couple of stupid men were coming along too."

When Chrissie had gone, Nona said, "That explains a lot of what we saw."

Pauline nodded. "A love triangle on vacation," she said, sadly.

The two days of excursions and visits following their arrival were, however, murder-free. The continuing smouldering glances and hurried evasive manoeuvrings to avoid unwelcome meetings between the love triangle's participants, kept Pauline and Nona amused but nothing more.

"Holiday romances are the best," Nona laughd, as she and Pauline watched Mrs. Oddfellow drag her husband away from another possible meeting with Chrissie, the witch.

"You know," Pauline said, "I think this time, because everything seems set for murder, we won't have one. All the other trips, the murder came out-of-the-blue."

"It's for the best," Nona said. "Travel agents will stop booking us if things were to continue as they were."

Chapter 3: October 31, Evening at the Cemetery

"Either they're putting on a good show for us," one of the tour participants said, pointing to a tombstone across the cemetery where a body was sprawled, "or someone's been partying too hard already tonight."

Nona and Pauline screwed up their eyes to see more clearly. In the darkness, with pools of yellow light from the few lamps in the cemetery, it did look like a real person and not a mannequin.

"That looks like Chrissie," Nona said, at last. "Same costume, anyhow."

"It would explain she wasn't here for the tour," Pauline replied. "If she's been partying, I mean."

The two sleuths made their way through the narrow lane between the graves until they arrived at the body.

"It is Chrissie," Pauline said, crouching down to see her face, "and she's not drunk. She's dead. She's been stabbed." Pauline signaled the tour guide to join them at the body.

Nona's hand dived into her pocket for her phone. "I'll call 9-1-1."

Jolene looked at Chrissie in horror. "Is she dead?"

Pauline nodded. "Yes, you'll need to gather up the group but keep them away from here. The police won't thank us for trampling all over the crime scene."

"But she didn't come on the tour," Jolene said. "We should leave. The police can interview us back at the hotel, if they want to."

Nona and Pauline exchanged glances, before Nona said, "That would be for the best. Pauline and I will stay, and the police can come to the hotel after they finish here."

Jolene hurried off to turn the group, who were drifting toward the body, and hustled them back out of the gate they came through.

"Was she attacked here?" Nona asked, crouching down beside Pauline.

"In the cemetery, I think, yes," Pauline said. "The streets are too busy for anyone to safely carry a body here."

"Didn't she say she was to meet someone who knew about this cemetery?"

Pauline frowned. "She did. She even told us who it was, but I hadn't heard of him, and I can't remember."

"Me neither," Nona said, "but one of the gang will know. They're not all as mature as us."

"There's nothing wrong with my memory," Pauline said, crossly. "It just wasn't interesting information, that's all."

Wailing sirens announced the arrival of the police and ambulances. "They're here," Nona said. "Do we tell them we can help or do this ourselves?"

"We could leave it to the police."

"As we say every time," Nona agreed, "but never do."

"I say we do it ourselves," Pauline said. "I get irritated at their disbelieving expressions and sarcastic remarks."

Nona nodded. "It is annoying, I grant you. But I like them behaving that way because then we get to see their sheepish expressions after we've solved the case before them."

"It doesn't compensate enough for me," Pauline said, as an officer arrived at the scene.

"Now, ladies," he said, "move away from the body and let our people check it out."

Pauline thought he might just be able to hear her teeth grinding together but he gave no sign of it. She and Nona walked away and into a pool of darkness caused by the trees shading the lamps. They watched in silence as the forensic team quickly secured the scene and began examining the area.

"They have this, Nona," Pauline said. "We should give the woman in charge our names and where we're staying and leave."

"No way," Nona said. "We listen in and learn what we can."

Their conversation, though exchanged in almost whispers, alerted the detective in charge and she made her way over to them.

"You're the two who found the body?" she asked, tersely It sounded like she was angry they'd disturbed her evening.

"That's us," Nona said.

"Why were you here?

"It's Halloween, this is a haunted cemetery, and we're on a tour," Pauline said.

"Where's the rest of the tour?" the detective asked, looking around.

"Back at the hotel," Nona replied. "We didn't think you'd appreciate everyone gawking," Nona said.

"They should have stayed," the woman said, frowning.

"Our hotel is within walking distance and a much better place to interview people," Pauline said. She told the woman the hotel and its address.

"Walking distance?" The detective queried, mockingly.

Pauline shook her head in dismay. This could be a long night.

"We're the ones who found the body," Nona said. "The others hadn't made it this far into the cemetery, so you have the only two useful witnesses right here."

"I decide who's useful," the detective said, signaling a police officer over to them.

"Give your statements to him and don't go until we've spoken again." She turned and walked back to the crime scene.

After the officer had written down their information, he reminded them what the detective said and returned to the crime scene leaving the two sleuths alone.

"You see," Nona whispered, "they want us to hear what they find. Maybe they picked up our sleuthing vibes. After all, this is a place where vibrations can be felt by those who are sensitive enough."

"I don't think that detective has a sensitive cell in her body," Pauline said, "but it does mean we have a ringside seat and the opportunity to learn more than we could have gleaned on our own."

ACKNOWLEDGMENTS

For my family. The inspiration they provide and the time they allow me for imagining and typing makes everything possible.

I'd also like to thank my editors, illustrator and the many others who have helped with this book. Without them, my books would look very sorry indeed.

ABOUT THE AUTHOR

I've always loved mysteries, especially those involving Agatha Christie's Miss Marple. Perhaps because Miss Marple reminds me of my aunts when I was growing up. But Agatha never told us much about Miss Marple's earlier life. While writing my own elderly super-sleuth series, I'm tracing her career from the start. As you'll see, if you follow the Miss Riddell Cozy Mysteries series.

However, this is my Bio, not Miss Riddell's, so here goes with all you need to know about me: After retiring, I became a writer and when I'm not feverishly typing on my laptop, you'll find me running, cycling, walking, and taking wildlife photos wherever and whenever I can.

My cozy mystery series begins in northern England because that was my home growing up and that's also the home of so many great cozy mysteries. Stay with me though because Miss Riddell loves to travel as much as I do and the stories will take us to the many different places around the world I've lived in or visited.

ALSO BY P.C. JAMES

On Amazon, my books can be found at the Miss Riddell Cozy Mysteries series page.

And for someone who likes listening to books, *In the Beginning, There Was a Murder* is now available as an audiobook on Amazon and here on Audible and many others, including:

Kobo, Chirp, Libro, Audiobooks, Scribd, Bingebooks, Apple , StoryTel, Nook, Hoopla

You can find even more books here:

P.C. James Author Page: https://www.amazon.com/stores/P.-C.-James/author/B08VTN7Z8Y

P.C. James & Kathryn Mykel: Duchess Series

GoodReads: https://www.amazon.com/P.-C.-James/e/B08VTN7Z8Y

Printed in Great Britain
by Amazon